THE CANNIBAL

THE CANNIBAL

BY

DAVID WILSON

Parrhesia PUBLISHING

DISCLAIMER

This is a work of fiction. Any references to, or descriptions of historical events, real people or real places are used fictitiously. Names, characters, and places are all products of the author's imagination.

DEDICATION

Dedicated to my brother and best friend, God rest his soul.

ACKNOWLEDGMENTS

My thanks to Leadership Books; particularly to
Mr. Michael Stickler Publisher.
And to Jerry Brewer, editor, who believed
in me when no one else did.

TABLE OF CONTENTS

A NOTE FROM THE PUBLISHER

There are currently 2.3 million people incarcerated in the United States of America. Twenty-five percent of the entire population of the United States has come into contact with the Justice System in some significant fashion. Once a young man enters the system even for a short term, he will likely spend the remainder of his days doing "Life on the Installment Plan" being locked-up multiple times throughout his lifespan.

Dave Wilson is one of those who was chewed-up as a young man and spit out as a senior citizen.

Life in Prison has a culture of its own—and its own approach to justice. Inside, it makes sense to "Lifers" to live under the harsh and sometimes brutal conditions of prison. It becomes their home and where they are most comfortable. It's referred to as being "institutionalized," and every prisoner experiences a little bit of that conditioning to some degree.

Dave Wilson is a fantastic storyteller who draws the reader into the true-to-life prison culture. A culture that takes humanity, survival, and leaders.

This book tells that story, that perspective, like no other.

It's this story we at Leadership Books want to see told, read, enjoyed, ... and appreciated.

MICHAEL STICKLER, Publisher

PROLOGUE

In the California Department of Corrections, inmates are housed by a point system, being level 1 through 4 and death row. I was level 3 or 4, also known as Max, and Super-Max, for my entire ten-year term. These higher levels house some very dangerous, very high-profile inmates, with an extremely high percent of lifers.

This is a story about one of those inmates—in fact, a cellmate I once had, who supposedly killed and ate his victims thus earning him the title "The Cannibal."

Risky as it may have been, I chose to write a dual story. One about "The Cannibal" and how he got to his place in time. The other, a story about living in a super-max prison, one of the worst.

As the story unfolds, you will find yourself slipping away from your previously sheltered idyllic point of view, and expanding your mind traveling through one man's insanity, and opening your eyes to life inside the American penal system, thus reaching an ultimate conclusion,

... one not easily forgotten.

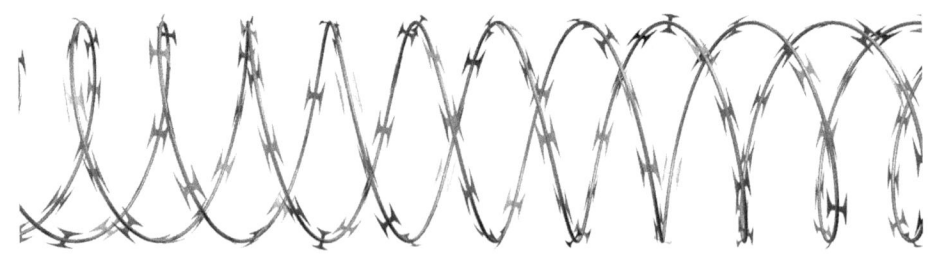

CHAPTER 1

SUDDEN DEATH

"Whoa … Whoa, you lost big guy?" my celly, Nathan, asked the huge black man named Tyrell, who just wandered across the weight pile and started pilfering our disc.

Tyrell ignored him and continued to collect pieces.

"You're a little out of bounds there, homey," Nathan persisted.

In the California Department of Corrections, known as the CDC, there are invisible lines, as real as the razor-wire itself. Blacks stayed on the east side and Whites on the west, keeping as much space between us as possible. The Hispanics claim territory somewhere in the middle.

The claim rang true everywhere; the chow hall, the building, visiting, even the chapel had some level of segregation. But the weight pile, it was an absolute. We didn't want to smell them, and the feeling was mutual.

Tyrell threw the weights to the ground, "What the fuck you gonna do about it, white boy?"

1

The yard froze in stunned disbelief.

Suddenly, Tyrell's head seemed to disappear as skin-head Tim came from nowhere and smashed a thirty-five-pound dumbbell straight through Tyrell's head, instantly freeing the big black buck of his short, chaotic life. Tim's actions triggered a chain of unimaginable pandemonium as the fluids of so many lost forgotten souls turned the whole weight pile into one big bloody mud pit.

From the comforts of my cell, I heard a half-dozen shots ring out.

Three hours later, when the guards marched the cut, bruised, and battered survivors back to their units, Nathan wasn't among them.

It didn't take long to realize; I needed a new celly.

With less than twelve months left to serve, the last thing I needed was another knucklehead, once again placing my release date in jeopardy. I headed to the yard to search ... for who?

Someone who didn't smoke. They had a TV, they were quiet, respectful, and preferably a lifer. For me, they were easier to live with. Generally, as a quiet, respectful person they would stay out of the mix. But, more than once, I've heard a lifer tell a youngster, "You may do that in county jail, but you don't do it here. I gotta live here."

To the yard, I went. My choices seemed limited.

Basically, if you needed a cell, that meant you'd been in the gym. The gym was one giant dorm. The only people who lived there were a few first-timers, some short-timers, and people coming out of the hole (knuckleheads).

While scouring the yard, I heard, "Dave!"

I spun around and found what seemed like the entire San Fernando Valley car approaching me. "What's up, guys?"

"I hear you've got an empty cell!" their shot-caller Kirk barked.

"Yeah ... I was just out here scoutin' around."

"Scout no further, my friend. We got a homeboy fresh out the hole, Trigger. Remember him?"

I remembered him alright. He is on his ninth prison term, heroin addict, tats all over his face, constantly fighting, currently coming back from a staff assault.

"Listen, guys; I'm getting short, kinda trying to stay out of the limelight. Ya know what I'm sayin'?"

"Yeah, yeah, whatever. Look, I'll get ya Trigger's number at the next unlock. You can give it to the CO, and we're good, right?"

"No, we're *not* good. You motherfuckers aren't moving nobody in my house. Do you see SFV blasted anywhere on me? No, ya don't. So, get the fuck off me!"

"Like that?"

"Yeah, like that. What I'm gonna do is look around, and if I don't find someone I want to live with, I'll get back to ya."

"I didn't mean no disrespect, dawg."

"Well, what do you call it? Like I said, I'll get back to ya."

On my way back to my cell, I passed the Dago car, my homeboys.

"Pac-man, you got a minute?"

"Yeah, Dave … What's up?" Pac-man, our shot-caller, asked as we walked a lap.

"I got SFV sweating me. I guess Trigger's coming out of the hole, and I don't want him."

"I already know. It's that Kirk motherfucker. That dude causes so much trouble."

"Yeah, ain't no thing. I already told him what's up. I'm just keeping you up to date."

"And I thank you for that. You move anybody into your cell you want."

"Listen, Pac-man, I know Tank's coming back to the yard soon ..."

"No, no, I got no hidden agenda, and I'm not trying to plant any seeds. Me and the homeboys already talked about it. You been here a long time Dave. It's time for you to go home."

"Thanks, P."

Ironically, San Diego didn't have a very big car here, but what they lacked in numbers, they made up for in brawn, despite the heroin and prison politics that continually tried to keep them down.

Time was running out. I knew soon the man would randomly select whoever was standing in line and curse me with his arrogant presence. That night after dinner, as much as I wanted to absorb the peace and solitude of single-cell-living, I drug myself back to the yard to further my search.

That's when it hit me. I was leaning against the chow hall wall, refreshing my mental checklist—unfortunately, with the two biggest junkies on the yard, Tank and Trigger, still hogging the top—when he calmly, quietly strolled by.

> Glen Sombers, a.k.a., "The Cannibal."
> Seven consecutive life sentences.
> Rumor has it he ate his victims.

Can you imagine how bad my life has become? Here I was considering living with a *cannibal,* a murderer, a monster, instead of a homeboy fresh out of the hole.

Ya, see, here's the thing. That homeboy, who no doubt can't wait to get back to the yard, back to his next shot of dope, is most likely going to get me in trouble. Whereas, the Cannibal, all I have to do is make sure he doesn't eat me. I can do that.

Well, plus, there's the issue of people hitting on him. The dude's been to the hole like … three times already this year. But, I think every time, it was for my bored homeboys lumping him up.

Youngsters in the pack get sent on these mini-missions just to keep them active. This is the exact reason Charley Manson could never walk a yard. Anyway, if I do this, that BS would have to stop.

I left my perch with several eyes on me and began closing the gap between us.

I've never seen a human being speak to Glen. Hell, for that matter, I don't even know if he talks! But, I mean, some monsters speak, right? I noticed the Dago car monitoring my every move. Glen had one earbud in and one ear open as I approached, obviously a futile attempt at survival.

I wasn't quite sure what to say as I kept pace a mere three feet to his side, slightly wowed by his six-foot, six-inch tall, lean frame.

"You smoke?" I finally asked.

Glen stopped and turned. I didn't see fear in his eyes, nor did I see a monster. He grinned and said, "No, why do you ask?"

"You no doubt have all your own shit, you know, TV and all, right?"

Glen's expression slightly changed, but the grin only widened. "Are you asking me if I want to move in?"

I paused, "Yeah, I guess I am. I mean, you gotta be getting sick of that fuckin' gym."

"I am … and yes, I would love a cell." He outstretched his hand, "I'm Glen, Glen Sombers."

"I know who you are, Glen. Everybody knows who you are. I'm Dave. Give me your number and pack your stuff. I'll go talk to the cop (CO) right now."

"Thank you, Dave."

Glen cut his lap short and headed back to the gym to wait for the next unlock. I didn't make it twenty feet before I noticed Pac-man and three other homeboys headed my way.

"Dave, dude—what the fuck?" Pac-man asked.

"What happened to 'anybody I want,' Pac-man?" I chuckled.

"*People*—Dave, you know, like human beings. Those kinda any bodies. Not the Cannibal."

"I know, Pac-man. But listen, guys, I'm tired, real tired. Tired of all this. I'm talkin' every motherfuckin' bit of it. … This dude looks like he might be pleasant, well, maybe not pleasant, but a change. Something different. Ya know what I'm sayin'?"

"We ain't sweatin' ya bro; we're just trippin' a little."

"Well, quit trippin'—Oh yeah … I'm gonna need ya all to stop beating on him too."

"Of course, Dave."

"Thanks. Hey, and if you guys don't see me around, feel free to come check, although there probably won't be much left to find!"

Everybody laughed awkwardly.

Glen moved in the following morning. When I got home from work, he and his belongings were neatly tucked away. He was on his rack, the top bunk with his headphones on, watching his TV—Dateline, it looked like, with his feet dangling off the end of the bed. The conversation was minimal, which I preferred, not because he's "The Cannibal," no, it was more like I'm tired, tired of it all.

I gotta say, that first night and possibly a few to follow, it was eerie, verging on creepy. The man didn't snore. He didn't even change his breathing pattern, meaning I couldn't tell if or when he was asleep.

Anyway, morning came, like all the others. Glen, having just come from the hole, was currently unassigned, no job, and wide awake with his headphones on, watching the morning news, when my alarm sounded. He knew how to do time, never getting in the way or making a sound, clean and respectful.

"So, how long you been down?" I asked.

"Thirteen years, give or take—you?"

"Only five, and until I met you, it sounded and felt like a long time."

Neither of us were big talkers, not in the cell anyway, but this idle chit-chat definitely broke the ice.

One night, probably day four or five, I was deep in a new episode of Seinfeld when Glen's face appeared over the edge of his bed.

"You have to be wondering?" he asked.

I removed my headphones. "Excuse me?"

Glen repeated himself.

"Well, sure, I'm a little curious."

He slowly pulled himself to a sitting position, started shuffling through his cubby-hole locker. I went back to my TV.

A few minutes passed. At the next commercial, Glen handed me down a manilla envelope and went back to his show.

After Seinfeld, I started reading.

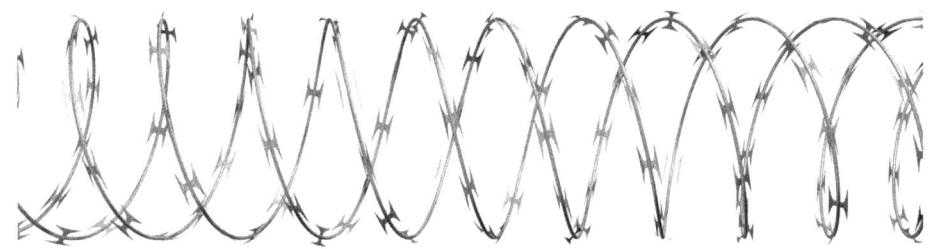

CHAPTER 2

THE PERFECT CELLY

The year was 1985. Glen, at age thirty-six, was a single, divorced bachelor who managed a True Value Hardware store located in a place called Lakeside, a suburb of San Diego.

His mother succumbed to breast cancer when he was just eleven. Basically, making his father, Tom, the single parent. These two were very close until Tom passed away while on vacation with his new wife in the Bahamas. Her name was Gloria. She had four kids, all boys and all grown.

One of Gloria's sons was a paralegal named Donny. Another, named Charley, thought he was a stockbroker. The third, Ricky, worked at a Safeway right down the street from the True Value. And last, but far from least, was Jason, who never worked a day in his life and truly believed mom and his new stepdad owed him the world.

Glen didn't see eye-to-eye with his stepmom or any one of her four sons. He tried—time and time again—knowing his father wanted them all to get along. Glen would set up dinners and other casual events, in which no one would ever show.

He couldn't put his finger on it. Something just wasn't right. The lack of feeling, the lack of love, once so abundant in his father's household, was now foreign to his father's life.

One day his dad called, "Glen, you open for lunch tomorrow. I have some things to go over with ya."

"Yeah, what's up, pops? Everything okay?"

Glen met his father at Applebee's the following day. He looked rough, with his hair, usually none out of place, dangling across his forehead. His clothes wrinkly, unkempt, possibly soiled.

"Dad, what's going on?"

Glen's dad signaled for him to sit down.

"Seriously, Dad, you don't look so good," Glen said the second he found his seat.

"I think she's trying to kill me. Her and those goddamned kids of hers."

"What?"

"I'm serious. I think she's putting stuff in my food and other weird things too … like my brakes on my truck went out last week."

"I remember you mentioned that."

"Yeah, well, the following morning, after I had it towed home, I found what looked like clean-cut brake lines."

"And you think she's poisoning your food?"

"I do. They don't eat the same food as me. She cooks special plates just for me. The other day that no-good, lazy son of hers."

"Jason?"

"Yeah, him. He accidentally almost ate out of a pot of spaghetti sauce, 'her special pot'—made just for me. You'd have thought Gloria saw a rattlesnake, the way she flew across the room."

"How you been feeling?"

"Horrible, sick all the time. Can't seem to keep a clear thought. I even lost my balance and fell like twice. That's not me. I don't fall. I'm telling ya, something's goin' on."

"How long have you felt this way?"

"See, that's the thing. About two, maybe three months ago," Glen's dad rubbed his head, "I took out a life insurance policy with you as the beneficiary. She's hounded me for weeks, then one day, she just stopped. So, yesterday I think it was my attorney, called and said he had a form he forgot about that I needed to sign to complete the transaction."

Tom paused to take a drink of water.

I asked, "'transaction'?"

"Yeah. 'It's no big deal,' he says, 'Let Gloria know I took care of it, will you please?'—I didn't know what to say, so I left it alone."

"Dad?"

"I know, but I wasn't sure what was going on yet. I'm still not."

He rubbed his head again.

"Then this morning, she's all smiles. First time I've seen her smile in months."

He hit his water again.

"All of a sudden, she's holding up these tickets, three of them."

"Three?" Glen asked ... skeptically.

"Yeah, three, for the Bahamas. Me, her, and that piece-of-shit son of hers. ... I don't get it."

"That is weird."

"I'm telling ya, she's never mentioned anything about wanting to go anywhere, much less the Bahamas."

Tom took another large gulp of ice water.

"See, like right now. Look at me. I'm flushed."

His face shiny, with a thin layer of oily sweat, he held out his shaky hands. "This isn't me. You know that, Glen."

"I do. Look, let me swing by, maybe talk to Jason, see what I can learn. You don't even need to be home, nor does anyone need to know about this meeting."

"When?"

"I don't know. Where's Gloria right now?"

"She gets her hair done today."

"Perfect. I'll call ya later, let ya know what happened."

I got up to take a leak. Facing the wall, apparently sound asleep, Glen's body slowly rolled up and down. '*Man, I wish that dude snored,*' I thought.

I sat back on my bunk. My clock read 12:48 a.m. Five in the morning rolls around pretty early. Intrigued, I continued to read.

Glen's father, Tom, Gloria, and Jason lived in Glen's childhood home near the Pacific Ocean, in Point Loma, California, fifteen minutes from downtown San Diego and two minutes from the infamous Ocean Beach.

Glen sat out front, taking it all in. The lawn he used to keep so pristine, now grown over and weed infested. The garage door he and his father repaired and or replaced several times, like the house, now chipped and faded.

All the curtains were closed. Glen looked up to his bedroom window. The curtain moved. Someone was definitely home. He approached the steps, snatching two old newspapers on the way. Savoring the moment, anticipating that old familiar chime, he pressed the doorbell.

Nothing.

Aggressively he beat on the door.

"Okay, okay, I'm coming!"

"Who is it?" Someone yelled through the crack.

"Glen."

The door opened on a chain.

"What do you want?—Your father's not here."

"Just wanted to have a word. You gonna invite me in?"

"No, I'm not. What do you want?"

"Can we talk?"

"No, get the hell out of here."

"Look, Jason, I don't know what you're up to, but it has to stop. You hear me. It has to stop!"

"You need to just mind your own business, buddy-boy."

"My dad is my business—asshole!"

Jason slammed the door.

"This isn't over!" Glen hollered on his way back to his car.

Startled, he nearly walked right into Gloria's car as it bounced up the driveway.

"What isn't over?" She rudely barked as she flew from the driver's seat.

"Listen, Gloria, I don't know what's going on here, but believe me, it's gonna stop."

"And just what is it, Glen? What is going on?"

"I don't know, but …"

"… But nothing, Glen. How 'bout you get yourself off my property before I call the police'."

"Your property?—the police?"

Jason opened the front door, "I told him, Mom, but he just wouldn't leave."

"Yes, *my* property. Soon they will all be *my* properties."

"What?—You're insane."

"Jason,—Call the police."

"No need. I'm leaving. Watch yourself, Gloria. You too, Jason!" Glen hollered toward the house.

"Are you threatening us?"

Glen hopped in his car and peeled out.

For the next day and a half, Glen called his father continually. Each time someone would answer, then hang up. '*I'm going there first thing in the morning,*' Glen told himself right before someone knocked at the door.

Not being a very social person, a visitor at 8:10 p.m. in the evening was not only unusual but uncalled for. Nevertheless, Glen reluctantly answered the door.

"Donny?" Standing just shy of the doormat was Gloria's oldest son, smiling from ear to ear.

"You've been served." He held out some papers. Glen slowly reached for them.

"Now—stay away from my mom!" He turned and shuffled away.

Glen kicked the door shut while looking at the letter—blasted across the top of page one in big, bold letters read—'**RESTRAINT ORDER.**'

Gloria, probably through Donny's legal resources, had somehow included her and her son Jason as owners of the properties, and not only the house Glen grew up in but also on him and his father's investment properties as well.

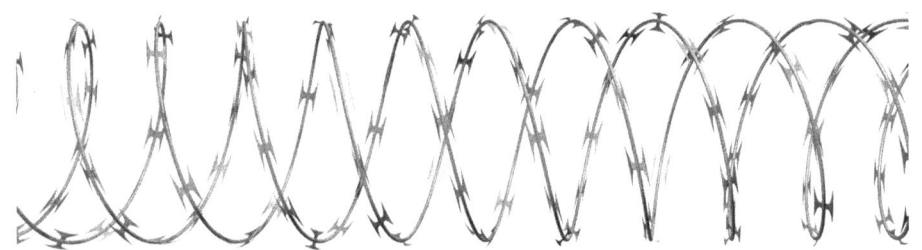

CHAPTER 3

LIVING WITH THE NOTORIOUS "CANNIBAL"

My clock read 2:58 a.m. I really needed to get some rest. I slipped his file back in its manilla envelope and closed my eyes. What felt like seconds later, my alarm went off.

Glen was quietly drinking coffee on his rack, watching the morning news. I jumped up, got dressed, and headed to work. All day I couldn't stop thinking about Glen and how did he possibly become a seven-time lifer, a *cannibal*?

Lunch came. I rushed to the chow hall like I do every day. There were certain benefits to getting there first. First, being somewhere among the first two hundred in line. Benefits, like hot food and knowing you're going to get your issue.

"Dave." I heard, after I grabbed my tray. Pac-man was waving me over to one of the white tables he and some homeboys secured.

"You got all your limbs, dawg? All your fingers? How 'bout your toes?"

Everyone chuckled.

"Maybe you guys should start worrying about him. I mean, you don't see his ass in here, do ya?"

People laughed.

"What the fuck you laughin' at?—I'm serious."

"On the real, dawg?" Pac-man asked.

"How is it? Is he a fuckin' weirdo or what?"

"I'm telling ya, Pac-man. It's only been a few days, but so far, he's one of, if not the best, celly I've ever had!"

"Wow, who'd a thunk?"

"I know, huh?—I'm reading his paperwork right now. Been up all night."

"No shit."

"Yeah, I haven't got to the murders yet or the other shit, but I'm tellin' ya, I can't wait to get back to it."

"You sure you want to know?" Pac-man asked.

"Fuck yeah."

I took my last bite.

"Gotta fly dawg. I'll see ya on the yard."

With no more fear of knuckleheads jumping him, Glen was gone when I got off work. I would later learn this is something he did daily just to give me my space. He showed up for count, got right on his bed, put on his headphones, and watched TV. Truly the world's best celly ever.

After count and chow, I went to work out. That night, tired with only a couple hours' sleep, I decided to continue his file tomorrow. Yeah, right—I reached for the envelope.

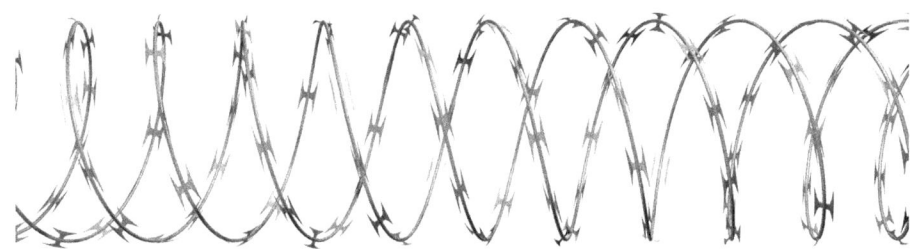

CHAPTER 4

GLEN'S REVENGE

Holding the restraint order, Glen thought to himself, *five hundred feet. How am I gonna do that?* The following morning, Glen went to see his attorney, who wasn't answering his phone. His office was closed. Glen checked back around noon. Still no luck.

He drove by his dad's. The place looked abandoned, with two more newspapers littering the front yard. At 4:45 p.m., his attorney's secretary finally answered the phone only to say, "Mr. Moor is in a meeting. Is there something I can help you with, Mr. Sombers?"

"Yeah, well, no, maybe not. This is an urgent issue. When can I catch him?"

"He has court the rest of this week, but I will leave him a message—wait, Mr. Sombers—I think I have something here for you to sign." She shuffled through papers, "Here it is—Oh, looks like it's been taken care of. I'll tell him you called."

"No—wait. What do you mean it's been taken care of? What's been taken care of?"

"I'm not sure, Mr. Sombers, but I will have Mr. Moor call you."

Violating a restraining order for a law-abiding citizen, such as himself, was out of the question. With no word from his father or attorney and neither one answering his calls, Glen was a complete wreck for the next week. Each day he drove by his father's house. Newspapers were building up. Mail covered half the front porch. Obviously, no one was around.

One day, with his stress levels nearly topping the charts, that dreaded call from the Bahamas came, that call Glen will never forget. His father, Thomas George Sombers, died at sea in an unfortunate boating accident … hyperventilating, the room began to spin. He grabbed his chest. It felt like a Mack Truck was sitting on him.

Suddenly, his head exploded, and gloom consumed him. For the next twenty-plus hours, Glen's unconscious body wallowed in its own waste. *Where am I?* Glen thought before he curled into a fetal position and wailed like the heartbroken man he was.

Cold, I'm so cold, wet. Is that urine? He slowly raised his hand to his nose and accidentally touched his cheek. *Have I soiled myself?* He looked around the room. *How long have I been lying here?* He tried to get up. His body refused to cooperate. One leg merely twitched on his command.

Glen shut his eyes and thought, *please, oh please, just make it go away*—before the darkness once again enveloped him. Several more hours passed.

'Bee—eep' his answering machine sounded for what seemed like the thousandth time. *Dad's attorney, What's his name? … Mr.? Why can't I remember his name?*

"Mr. Sombers, this is Mr. Moor, your father's attorney for the estate. I've been trying to reach you for days."

That's it—Moor!

"I understand your father is on vacation in the Bahamas. Anyway, about two weeks ago," … papers shuffled, "Here it is, … September twenty-ninth, … he changed the executor of his will to Gloria, his wife, basically relinquishing any and all debts and or business you previously secured with our firm. Mr. Sombers. if you have any questions and or wish to do business with us in the future, please feel free to contact my office. I believe you have the ... "

"I'm going to kill her!"

"What! Hello, hello, Mr. Sombers? ... Glen? ... are you there?"

The line went dead.

Uncertain exactly what he heard; the attorney failed to report the threat.

Fueled by revenge, Glen pulled himself to an upright position and looked around the room. Once so familiar, now unrecognizable ... *the colors, where did they come from?* The carpet, wiry and itchy to his feet. The picture of his dad and him fishing in Baja ... *Who are those people?*

He tried to weep. Nothing came out but the dust left by his aching soul. Glen swore that moment to never cry again in his life.

Led only by instinct, he stumbled toward the shower, leaving a light trail of small feces chips behind. The hot water was wide open, the cold untouched, as the bathroom filled with steam.

Glen shook uncontrollably to the freezing ice pellets that seemed to cut through his skin.

What's wrong with me? he thought as he sat with his knees pulled to his chin, watching the water empty through the drain. *Revenge ... that's right, revenge.*

Glen got up, turned the hot water off, and walked out of the bathroom, dripping water as he went. *Dad's service pistol.* He headed to the den, to his glass hutch, the one he and his father filled with memories long past, now so foreign to him.

The weapon felt heavy in his hand. *Was it always this heavy?* Glen wondered. *I don't think I've ever touched it.*

Food,—maybe I should eat. What do I like? Am I even hungry?

Naked and confused, Glen walked to the kitchen, by the phone machine. Twenty-seven messages. He hit "delete," and continued toward the kitchen, with the gun limply swinging by his side. After preparing a pickle sandwich, nothing else, just one large dill pickle, he thought to himself, *Do I even like pickles?*

He grabbed a pen and paper out of the junk drawer and plopped down at the kitchen table, nearly smashing his nuts as he sat. Gloria topped his list. Followed by Jason, 'the asshole.' Donny 'served him papers.' Ricky ... *and while I'm at it, Charlie will have to go too. All five must die.* Glen thought as he took a bite of his sandwich.

Okay, how will I do it?

Glen finished his strange lunch, got dressed, and walked to his car, slightly dragging his right foot. He went to the army surplus store in El Cajon, a few miles from his house. Not quite sure what he was looking for, he moseyed around the store, eventually locating a Soldier of Fortune Magazine, and headed for home.

Unlocking the door, he heard 'Bee—eep' "Glen, this is John, from work. Where have you been? Are you okay? We're starting to worry about you. Tim fired you tod ..." 'Bee—eep'…

Not quite sure who John from work was, or for that matter, where exactly he performed this work, Glen ignored the call.

For some reason, unknown to him, Glen was naked again, now reading his Soldier of Fortune Magazine. Page 63, "*Ten Most Deadly Cocktails.*" It sounded like a good place to start.

After a thorough review of this section and all its ingredients and potions, Glen leaned toward a toxic crystalline substance, created by some seemingly simple ingredients, all of which should be readily available right here in town. This powder could be sniffed, drunk, eaten, smoked, or injected—basically, all forms of ingestion.

Once ingested, within twenty minutes, paralysis of the limbs sets in, rendering its victims immobile. Shortly thereafter, the lungs cease to function while the heart slows to a trickling pace. Sleep, *which is just too good for them,* consumes the victim before they succumb to the inevitable—death.

"Perfect," Glen said as he placed the magazine on the couch beside him. "Now, just to figure out how?"

For the next week, never answering his phone or door for anyone or anything. Glen hunted chemicals and worked on his plan.

Home Depot was the hot spot. He located all but one, something called selenium sulfate. He went to the local library and researched. Apparently, selenium sulfate is De–Chlor ... simple De–Chlor ... for fish tanks.

Glen headed to Fontains on El Cajon Boulevard and found said chemical with ease, for $4.99. "Wow, less than five bucks!" Glen told himself on his way home.

He started with three buckets. That's what the magazine said. He poured half a gallon of sulfuric acid in one, one pint of De–Chlor, with a quart of a concrete cleaning solvent in another—this mixture hissed.

While adding ice (according to the magazine), he quickly poured six cans of Red Devil lye—the ingredients said one half a can. Once again, violating said portions, he added twelve cans of De–Con rat poison, instead of the recommended one. Boiling, popping, and smoking, the vile rainbow-colored substance quickly rose to the bucket's rim. The smell of a million rotten eggs nearly buckled Glen's knees. He choked and ran for the mask he bought at Home Depot.

When he returned minutes later with the mask now secured in place, the substance, although still active had seemed to settle. Glen continued to add ice. This calmed the mixture, as the magazine said it would.

Once the bucket was cool to the outside touch, he was to pour the half-gallon of sulfuric acid in. The magazine said to be careful and stand as far back as possible. Glen did this. The substance popped and boiled, sending splashes of toxic waste onto the linoleum floor, eating it instantly.

Now, in one big finale, Glen quickly poured the entire concoction into the final bucket, where a block of dry ice lay silently lurking.

BOOM!—The fireless explosion threw Glen across the room—headfirst into the wall.

Suddenly everything stopped. There was no reaction of any kind as Glen's ears rang. Smoke floated in mid-air causing a cloud–type effect throughout the entire house.

Glen pulled himself off the ground and slowly approached the seeming disaster. The bucket was empty? Nothing, not even residue, remained.

Confused, Glen dropped the bucket to the floor. Inside, the bucket's content shattered like glass, fracturing into crystal clear, glass shards. Glen picked the bucket back up.

It was about one-quarter full—of what? He wasn't sure. And with no real way to test it, he would have to rely on *Soldier of Fortune Magazine*. Why not? Everything worked like they said so far?

The article concluded with "a hundredth part of a grain of this tasteless odorless substance could potentially kill 200–plus people." That meant he had enough of this wicked concoction to destroy nations! The feeling was empowering, to say the least.

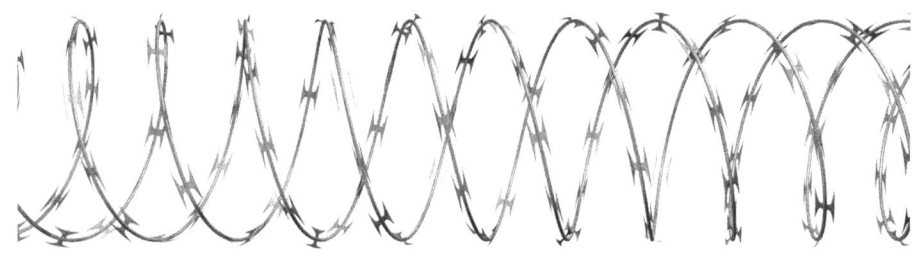

CHAPTER 5

POLITICS

Saturday morning prison life was basically whatever you wanted it to be. In general, the guards run an easy crew, being their Captain and usually anyone else hell-bent on ruining your life is at home with their families, not searching your cell and destroying your meager belongings. Truth be known, the Captain actually runs the prison.

I read Glen's story until close to 4:00 a.m. I slept all the way to 10:00 a.m. Glen was gone when I woke.

After a hot cup of coffee, I headed to the yard to burn some laps. Tank was waiting outside the sally port.

Similar to its sister sally ports across the world, you quickly realize a prison sally port differs in one big way. As you are squeezed through the narrow, cinder block tunnel and glance up through the clear glass ceiling, you see two armed guards staring down at you, making this one of, if not the most, dangerous place on the yard.

"Dave, ... What's up dawg?"

"Hey, Tank … Heard you were coming back soon."

"Yeah, they let me out late yesterday. They can't pin that shit on me. I mean, I hit the motherfucker—don't get that fucked up, but the dope? That could have been anybody's."

"Dope?"

"Ain't no thing. Anyway, I heard The Cannibal's your celly."

"Yeah, I moved him in last week or so."

"Okay. … Well, get rid of him. I need a cell, *home ... boy*."

"Listen, Tank, with all due respect, that's not gonna happen."

"What!"

"Ya see, I didn't stumble on him. I purposely moved him in."

"Why?"

"I'm tired, Tank. I'm done fuckin' around. I'm over all this bullshit."

"Yeah, well, what's that got to do with me needing a place to live?"

"Look, Tank …"

"… Look my ass!" Tank yelled, "Get that fuckin' lame out of there and let me know soon as you do." Tank tried to walk away.

"Check this out, Tank.—What the fuck you think I am?— talking to me like that!"

Tank spun around, "Talk to you like what, homeboy?"

Pac-man rolled up in the nick of time … "Guys, guys, settle down. I already told you where it's at, Tank. What's wrong with you?"

"Whatever," Tank mumbled as he stomped away.

"Homeboy or not, I don't like that dude. And I'm so glad he's *not* my new celly."

Pac-man laughed, "Yeah, me too, dawg."

I went on to catch my morning laps, with Tank "mad doggin" me each time I passed his way.

"You got a problem, Tank?" I asked.

"No, I'm good."

23

"Well then, quit lookin' like you do."

The yard recalled for lunch. After lunch, Glen once again headed out, and I continued to read.

... Three hours later, Glen's head and body pounded to the erratic beat of his heart while stomach bile shot out his nose, as he painfully purged his pickle sandwich lunch. Naked, he laid on the bathroom tile, fading in and out of consciousness ... waking only to moan, hold his head, and dry heave. ...

———————◆ ◆ ◆ ◆◆◆ ◆ ◆ ◆———————

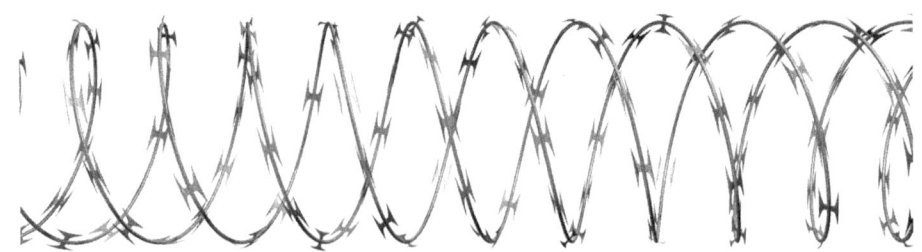

CHAPTER 6

'TOXIC SATURATION'

After two days of bleeding out his nose, eyes, ears, penis, and ass, Glen wasn't sure if he was going to live or die. He hoped for the latter. Waking on the third day, completely depleted of any and all bodily fluids, he crawled to the shower.

"I hurt too much to be dead," he told himself as he drug his limp body to bed. His head rang, his stomach tied in knots, his skin lumped and blistered. "Will it ever stop?" his breathing became erratic, his heart beat faster and faster. His whole body shook violently before he fell into a dark deep comatose-type sleep.

Twelve hours later, Glen opened his eyes and groaned, lying on his soiled, cold, sweat-soaked mattress, dehydrated, and completely depleted of all nutrients. He was desperately sick and basically sore all over, and in need of some vitamins, to say the least.

Falling in and out of consciousness he tried to get dressed. After several failed attempts, he managed a shirt and pants. He couldn't bend to deal with shoes.

He had two swollen black eyes now blood red where the whites used to be. His hair had greyed overnight and missing in spots. Overall, he looked like a dead–man walking.

His goal? Walgreens, less than two miles away. Two very long miles, in which he nearly crashed twice. Wishing he had crutches, he parked as close to the front door as possible and hobbled into the store. Once inside, he grabbed a shopping cart for stability and in a no–nonsense manner began collecting his needs. That's the last thing he remembered.

Beep … Beep … Beep …

Glen cracked an eye, that now was almost swollen shut.

Beep … Beep … the monitor sounded.

The hospital. I'm definitely in a hospital. Alone, with the curtains closed, he tried to rise. His head pounded. His body was weak, real weak.

The curtain drew to the side. "Mr. Doe, do you know where you're at?" The male nurse asked.

Glen winced when he tried to shake his head.

"Just lay still. You're in Grossmont Hospital's emergency room. Do you know what happened?"

"No," Glen groaned.

"Apparently, you passed out in Walgreens."

The nurse shuffled some papers. "Do you know your name?"

Glen didn't answer.

"Okay then, Doe it is. So, John, do you have any idea how you became such a mess?"

Glen once again stared at the ceiling. Before passing back out.

He woke the next day to a female nurse drawing his blood. "Mr. Doe, glad to see you're still with us."

Glen's head and body still ached.

"You had a very rough night. You actually flatlined twice. Do you remember any of it?"

"No."

"Do you remember your name?"

"No."

"Okay, the doctor will be in soon. Hang in there, Mr. Doe." The nurse said on her way out of his room.

"What's your name?" the old man in the next bed grumbled.

Startled, Glen once again winced as he turned his head to the side, a task he couldn't perform yesterday. With his single eye now back on the ceiling, Glen growled, "Glen, name's Glen."

"Robert," the old man groaned.

The door opened.

"Mr. Doe," a man in a white lab coat, carrying a clipboard, said, "I'm Doctor Simpson. Do you have a name?"

"… Mark? … Mark Miller?"

The doctor wrote it down. "Okay, Mr. Miller. Two days ago, you were brought in by way of an ambulance. You were in very bad shape. We've done a series of tests and determined you've been poisoned. Although we can't seem to identify its nature. Do you have any idea wha…?"

". . . No."

The doctor stared.

"Okay, well, I think you're going to live, and that's something we weren't so sure about when you got here. But you're going to have to take it easy."

Glen didn't show any sign of recognition.

"Some people want to talk to you. I've stalled them long as I can. They'll probably be back tomorrow."

"Have I had a stroke?"

"Pardon me?"

"A stroke, heart attack, anything like that?"

"No, not that the tests show. You're suffering from some type of toxic saturation. But I find no sign of stroke or heart attack."

"When can I leave?" Glen growled.

"Well, Mr. Miller, you're lucky to be alive, so at this point, let's just take it one day at a time."

After the doctor left, Glen, still counting ceiling tiles, asked his roommate, "excuse me, Bob."

"Yeah?" the old man replied.

"What size shoe do you wear?"

Glen painfully sat up and pulled out his IV. Every joint, muscle, and bone ached to his every move. Even his teeth hurt. But his main problem was his head; it felt like an atomic bomb went off, leaving only mush in its wake.

"You need a couple bucks?" Bob asked.

"I guess it couldn't hurt. Left my wallet at home."

"Yeah, I figured that."

Bob's shoes fit, a little tight, but they'll work. Glen tried to stand upright and winced.

"You sure you wanna leave?"

"I have no choice, my friend. I'll repay ya for your hospitality once I get home."

"At this point, I'm not sure you're going to make it home, so don't worry about it."

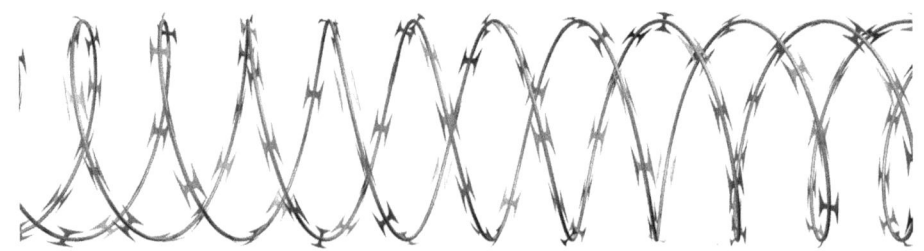

CHAPTER 7

TRIGGER-HAPPY BROOKS

In level three and four, your cell door opens every forty-nine minutes, for one minute, then nine minutes later for one minute, all day long, a.k.a. 'ten-minute unlocks.' This gives you time, so they believe, to go to the yard, class, work, shower, whatever.

During one of those unlocks, Glen came home … looking upset, scared maybe. I'm not sure, but basically uneasy. I sat down his file and asked, "What's up, dude?"

Failing to answer, he slowly removed his laundry bag from the wall and began stuffing his things in it.

"What are you doing?" I asked.

"Umm … I have to go."

"What do you mean, you have to go?"

"I don't want any trouble, so I'm gonna move back to the gym."

"What did Tank say?"

29

"Tank?"

"Yeah, my big homeboy. What did he say?"

"Look, I don't want any trouble."

"No, there's no trouble. Ya, see Glen, that dude is a super asshole. He's not running shit! Everybody's cool with you living here. Even if you weren't here, I wouldn't move that jerk in. So, on the next unlock, I'll go deal to his dumb ass."

Glen stood there holding his laundry bag.

"Put that shit down. You're not going anywhere."

"I just don't want to cause any trouble."

"And you're not—Tank is." I said, as I started placing my more precious things on my bed, things I didn't want to lose when the CO came to pack my stuff.

"Listen, Glen, what I need is for you to hold down the house, so when I get out of the hole, I don't have to live in the gym. If the man moves someone in here, let them know they have to go when I get back. Got it?"

"Yeah, I got it. I just don't like you having to stick up for me."

"I'm not! I'm sticking up for me. Tank is directly disrespecting me. Actually, he's disrespecting our rep, Pac-man, me, and the whole Dago car. This shit can't go unchecked."

What I later learned was that Tank had barked "I don't give a fuck what the rep, Dave or any other motherfucker said, you're moving, and you're moving today! You hear me, stupid?"

I stood at my door patiently waiting for the key, who was only a few cells away. Yeah, I was nervous, Tank's a big dude. Then ya got a bunch of crazy-ass guards with M16s in multiple towers across the yard just dying to shoot someone, a.k.a. me.

But hey, I didn't get to prison by being scared, and today would probably be a bad time to start. So off to the yard I marched.

As I came out the sally port, I noticed a cloud of dust surrounding the Dago car. I picked up my pace.

Uncertain who or how many were involved, people ran from all over the yard.

Ya see that's how it happens. One second you're working out, or deep in a game of pinochle, and the next, you're getting your cap pealed in the middle of the full-blown riot.

As I ran, I saw Pac-man throw a haymaker that caught Tank right square in the nose. Both men were scuffed up, but at this early juncture, Pac-man appeared to be on top.

Peww … The shot echoed across the hillside. Tank spun, hitting his head on a concrete bench on his way to the ground.

Peww … The second shot rang out. Pac-man threw his hands on top of his head and dove for the ground.

Peww … The third and final shot blared, catching him somewhere in his upper body on his way down.

Then—and only then—the alarm sounded. We all hit the ground. Anyone not completely flat to the earth gets shot.

There are signs all around, "**NO WARNING SHOTS FIRED**," and on this day, they meant it.

COs came running from everywhere, as they always do. Two hours later, after they removed Tank's body, which was dead before it hit the ground, and rushed (what a joke) Pac-man to the hospital, where he'll be treated, and if he lives, eventually be returned to the yard, we were escorted back to our cells, unit by unit.

Did Tank deserve to die? I think a better question would have to be: Is the world a better place without him? Probably so.

Will his poor mother's heart ever mend? Probably not. But, hey, welcome to prison life.

Glen was standing at the cell door when I got back.

"I thought it was you," he said as I entered the cell.

"Yeah, it actually could have been, with that trigger-happy Brooks in the tower. But it looks like Pac-man beat me to it. I think Tank's dead."

"What about your friend?"

"Pac-man? I'm not sure where he got hit, but I think he'll be okay. He's too damn ornery to die!"

Glen smiled.

"Bottom line, the problem's gone, and it looks like we're gonna be on lockdown. At least until they investigate. I don't know about you, but I've got some reading to do!"

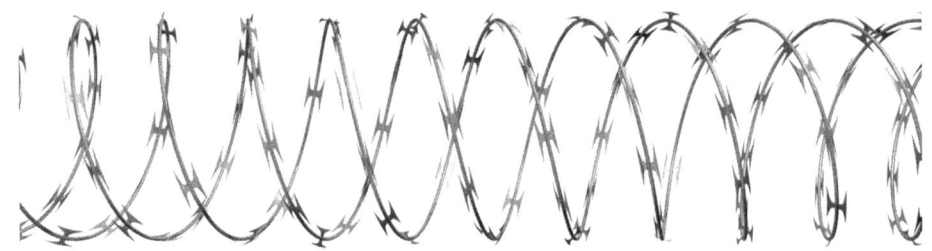

CHAPTER 8

RECUPERATING WHILE
REAFFIRMING REVENGE

Bob's shoes on, Glen grabbed his clothes off a nearby chair, dressed, and made his exit out of the hospital. Less than an hour later, a cab dropped him at his car, which fortunately was still sitting in Walgreen's parking lot. He drove straight home.

His house stank like rotten eggs. The walls were now discolored with rusty nail stains, showing through the drywall. The carpet was burnt, soiled, and missing in spots, exposing the bleached white concrete floor below.

"How long have I been gone?" he asked himself as he ventured around the house assessing the damage.

The kitchen, the bathroom, all wasted with rusty fixtures and burnt orange countertops. It seemed the only thing not damaged was the crystal-clear crystalline substance that sat untouched in the bucket, where it lingered with anticipation to exact Glen's revenge.

He quickly shut the door and exhaled.

For the next week he took it easy. Some cleaning, laundry washing, carpet extracting, nothing too major. He was more concerned about recontamination than he was getting the house in order. A house he no longer had any use for. A house that most likely now belonged to Gloria.

Nothing matters, except what I have to do. How, how will I do it? He thought—*the water. I'll contaminate their water. But how?*

Still recovering, the following morning, Glen limped outside to get today's paper. There it was in bold print. His father was truly gone and scheduled to be buried on Thursday, less than two days away.

Wasn't anyone even gonna tell me? Who? Gloria, one of her sons? I guess not.

He continued reading. His name was mentioned once, Gloria's six times, with a heartwarming statement from her. *'Give me a break!'*

"The grieving widow ..." the obituary read. It went on and on ....

Glen grabbed the phonebook and called one of those "free consultation" attorneys.

"No, Mr. ... Sombers ... was it? If there's an active restraining order against someone, they cannot, under any circumstances, violate the order. Not even for a funeral."

"So, who can't go, her or me?"

"Well, if *she* filed the order, *you* have to leave, even if you arrived first."

"That's not right."

"Be it right or not … it's the law."

For the next two days, Glen laid around often wondering if the contamination levels in the house were possibly hampering his recovery. Failing to do anything about it, he continued to channel-surf, naked on his chemical-stained couch.

While his body withered, so did his already compromised mind. Often, he watched silly infomercials or hours of grey particles long after TV viewing was over. Tomorrow was the funeral.

Rummaging through his closet, he couldn't figure out the proper attire. "No one will probably see me anyway," he told himself. "Did I used to wear these? Do they even fit?"

He selected a pair of blue slacks that were a little short, a yellow, long-sleeve shirt, and a pair of red tennis shoes. "No, no, this is all wrong," he said to the man in the mirror.

Back to the closet he went. "Why is this so hard?"

Eventually, he settled with a black-on-black, Johnny Cash-looking get-up that would become his daily attire. His hair was a mess … grey, black, bald spots in odd places. So, he shaved his head.

"What do you think?" he asked himself while staring into the mirror. Glen paused a moment, waiting for a reply, "Okay, be like that."

He cinched up his shirt's top button and hastily headed out.

"What's this?" … Glen snatched the paper from off his front door.

"Notice of Eviction? … You gotta be kidding me!" It was signed by Gloria herself.

Here it was. The day of his father's funeral. His father, who was dead because *SHE* killed him. And now, this.

He wadded up and threw the paper to the ground on his way to the car. The plan was to find a nearby hill at least 500 feet away, according to the order, and watch the ceremony with his binoculars. As silly as it sounded, coming from a man who was planning a mass homicide, he still didn't want to bring unnecessary attention to himself, potentially compromising his mission. The main mission. The only mission that mattered.

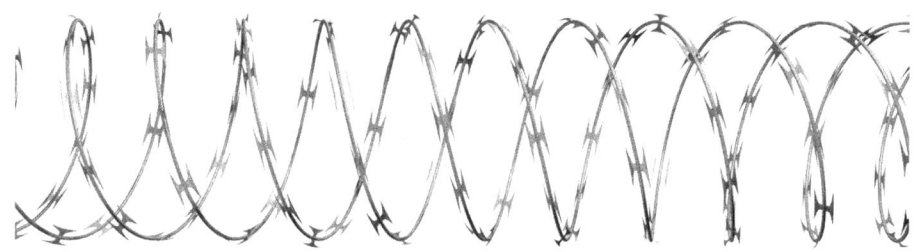

CHAPTER 9

LOCKDOWNS

"Chow–time," bellowed the guard seconds before the metal food slot dropped. First one tray, followed by a quick second, skipped into the cell. "Whoa, whoa, ... Wilson, you okay in there? When did they move *him* in?"

"They didn't. I did. And yes, I'm fine."

"Wait. What? Why?"

"Sombers, you're not hungry, are ya? ... the guard chuckled.

"Give it a break, boss … we're good."

"You must get tired of that?" I asked once the guard passed.

"Naw, I'm used to it."

Reading about how unstable Glen had obviously become, combined with the mere nature of his crime made me wonder how he could seem so sane. Wait, I think I may have read that somewhere—how some really crazy people can act normal when they need be.

I looked up at Glen, who even ate his meals on his bunk. A mysterious grin creased his face as if he read my mind. Goosebumps ran up my arm. This was the first uneasy moment, if you could call it that, since he moved in.

"You okay?" he asked.

"Yeah, I'm good. Why wouldn't I be?" ... "Are *you* okay?"

Glen smiled and continued eating.

Minutes later the guard returned for the trays, this time with a friend.

"Sombers, you want some extra food, or did Wilson give ya his?" the guard laughed.

"Yeah, yeah, whatever. How long we supposed to be down, boss?" I asked.

"Captain said for the rest of the day. You hear that Sombers? We should have ya out in the morning, so don't do nothing crazy, like eat your celly!"

The guards laughed all the way down the tier.

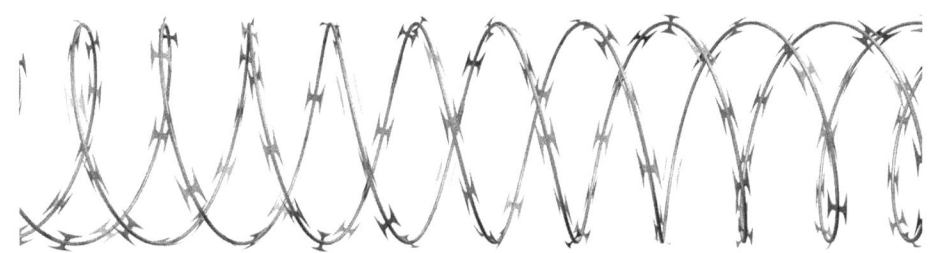

CHAPTER 10

THE FUNERAL

G len arrived at the cemetery an hour early. He parked just over a knoll nearest his mother's grave, then hiked a short distance with binoculars slung around his neck. After selecting his perch, he unfolded a small lounge chair and popped a corona, his father's favorite brew.

Minutes later the caravan began to arrive. At one point, with the ceremony well under way, Glen glanced across the crowd and noticed his Aunt Susan staring at him. Susan was his father's only sibling, and about six years younger than Thomas. Making an effort to be discreet, he lowered the binoculars and stood up. Susan backed out of the crowd and in a loop came Glen's way.

"What are you doing?" she asked.

Glen raised the binoculars back to his face, "I'm watching my father's funeral."

"I can see that. Why aren't you down there?"

"I can't." Glen mumbled under his breath.

"What?"

Finally, he lowered the binoculars. Then, turning to look at her, he said, "I can't, Aunt Susan. She has a restraining order against me."

"Who does?"

"Gloria! Do you know Dad supposedly changed his will recently, leaving her *everything*, including his and my investment properties?"

"Bullshit!"

"No," Glen stood up "The other day I went there to talk with her, an argument broke out and she filed a restraining order against me."

"Are you kidding me, Glen?"

"Dad told me a couple weeks ago he thought she was trying to kill him."

"Glen."

"I'm serious."

"Kill him?"

"Yes, well, not exactly in those words, but ...."

"Stop it!" She barked. "You sound like a lunatic right now."

"Maybe I am. Maybe this whole damn thing is making me a little crazy."

"Stop it Glen, please. We all miss Tom. I've been crying for two weeks. But we have to hold it together."

"I'm trying to tell you what's going on, and you're refusing to accept it."

"No, I'm not! I'm just finding it a little hard to believe, is all. But I promise you, I'll look into it."

Glen sat back down in his little chair and raised the binoculars to his face. "I'm not going to let her and her asshole sons get away with it. I know she's responsible for this. I can't prove it, but I know it."

"I know."

"Who told you about the funeral?" Glen asked

"Gloria did. Why?"

"No one told me anything."

"She told me you were the first one she called."

"I saw it in the paper … the *paper* Aunt Susan!"

"Are you gonna be okay, Glen?"

"Ha," Glen chuckled. "I'm gonna be fine. It's not *me* you should be worried about."

"Don't do anything stupid, Glen."

"I got an eviction notice this morning—out of my own house!"

"How?"

"I don't know. She's forging signatures or something. I'm not sure."

"I have to get back down there. Listen, Glen, I'll look into all of this. Meanwhile, please don't do anything stupid. Promise me?"

"Define stupid," Glen said from under the binoculars.

"Stupid, crazy, you know what I'm saying, Glen. Promise me." Susan said as she turned and walked away. Glen simply raised his Corona, giving it a little shake, and murmured "Dad's favorite brew".

He continued to watch the proceedings until all mourners had left. With one corona left, he walked down the knoll to pay his final respects. The backhoe had yet to move the dirt that in Glen's mind, would somehow seal his father's fate forever.

"I brought you a Corona."

Glen placed the beer in the hole.

"They're not going to get away with this, Pops. I promise you that. Whatever it takes and no matter what. I have to do this."

Glen listened.

"I know it won't bring you back, but something has to be done. Dad, please. Is this how you want me to remember you? Us arguing?"

Glen looked around.

"Listen Dad, I love you very much, but if you're not on board here, then I'll do it on my own!"

Glen started to leave "You stop it! You sound like Aunt Susan right now. I have to go. Enjoy your beer— Okay, okay, I'm sorry— your Corona."

As he walked back up the little hill he thought, *will I ever cry again? Probably not.*

Thirty minutes after he got home, he was once again naked and nauseated, with a pounding headache. The funeral was the first time he actually took in some fresh air. The house was obviously still contaminated.

Last night Glen stumbled outside and picked up the eviction notice that still laid crumpled in the yard. "Thirty days— are you kidding me? I *dare* her. Come to think about it, I won't even need thirty days."

He sat up most the night formulating his plan. "I'm gonna need a car. One they won't recognize."

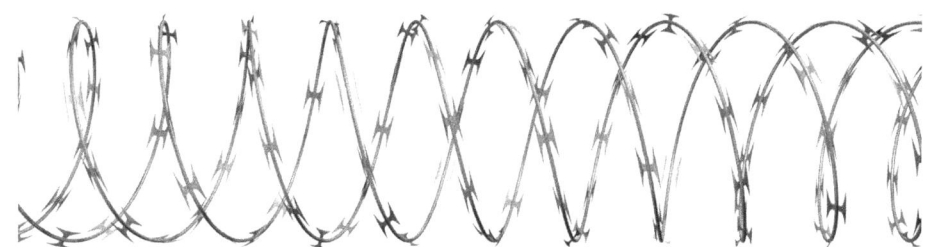

CHAPTER 11

DAVE TAKES ONE FOR THE TEAM

For some, Sunday's prison life was long, lonely, and boring. Most the jobs were shut down for the weekend. The entire education department closed. But the worse was the mail. Nothing came in or went out.

Basically, aside from a handful of people, particularly lifers, folks laid around their cells and thought about their families, their dog, their truck, and freedom. This is referred to as Hard–Timing.

Me, I stayed busy with my art, writing, exercise, and reading. Hard timing didn't look like much fun, so I chose not to do it. Well, little as possible, anyway.

After breakfast, today being cinnamon rolls, the only day I go, I went to the yard to check the aftermath. The Dago car was waiting.

"Dave, meeting in ten minutes—south bench," a homeboy named Brian barked.

"Yeah, I figured as much."

With my steaming coffee in hand to combat the early morning chill, I cut across the yard.

Brian voiced the groups' opinion. "Dave, Thanks for coming. Me and some of the fellas were talking."

"Here we go," I murmured under my breath.

"Just hear us out bro," Shorty, Brian's celly asked.

"Look, Dave, we know you're getting short to the house, but we need you to step up. Just until Pac-man gets back, or we can vote someone in."

"What's wrong with you, Bri?"

"CO swung by our house last night," Shorty chimed in, "said for neither of us to even think about it." Even though we ran the joint, the cops often let it be known; they were in control.

"We got plenty of soldiers, bro," Brian said.

"Pac-man didn't have to deal with Tank. He insisted on it."

"No, I get it. Like you said, I'm getting short. But don't trip. I'll take one for the team." This would prove to be one of the worse calls I ever made.

Less than an hour later, SDSH (San Diego Skin Heads) were at my door.

"Crunch, what's up, dawg?" I asked.

Crunch stood six feet seven and a half inches. He had to bend to walk in a cell.

"Not much," he said as he watched both directions down the tier.

"Heard you're filling in a minute."

"Unfortunately, I am. What can I help you with?"

Crunch chuckled.

"Listen, dawg, we're hitting Donny tomorrow afternoon. Have your homeboys step clear."

Not that it required one, but before I could reply, Crunch was gone.

I don't even know what Donny did. Rumor had it he owed for heroin. Not my concern, being he wasn't from San Diego.

I shot word by way of a porter and didn't even have to leave the cell.

It seemed like every few minutes, someone was on my door. People needed permission for this, a pass for that. So, and so isn't paying his bill, what should we do? "Cut them off," was my most common reply.

This went on through the evening. Some of which were life and death situations others were so stupid, so juvenile, they didn't even merit an answer.

"I don't know how Pac did this, day in and day out," I said to Glen, who smiled and made no comment. At one point, I actually found myself wishing the skinheads would hurry up and hit this Donny dude just so we'll be back on lockdown.

Filled with emotions, sleep was restless. Does so and so deserve the penance I have sworn against him? Did I let this other dude off too light? Clearly, this was not the job for me.

Like clockwork the following day, with me, Glen, and the entire Dago car either at work or comfortably stashed out in our cells, the shots rang out, followed by the alarm, as usual, exactly in that order.

Lockdown. Time to read

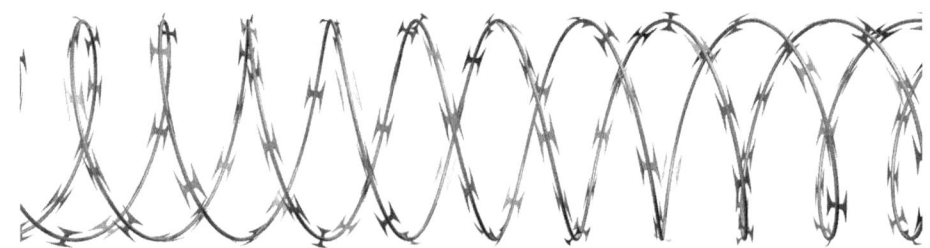

CHAPTER 12

FORMULATING HIS DEADLY BREW

Glen knew Gloria's birthday was coming up in about two weeks. His plan, although still a little sketchy, was to sneak in her house, "her house?" ... Dad's house ... when no one was home, and insert his deadly concoction, (his stomach turned whenever he thought about it) into her water purification canister, under the kitchen sink. That should do it.

"How to get in the house?" He asked himself.

He rented a car from Hertz and parked a comfortable block away, where he could monitor her and her son Jason's every move. He was looking for a pattern, something they did daily. For the entire first day of this recon mission, he saw little to no movement.

On day two, at 2:37 in the afternoon, Gloria, covered in sweats from head to toe, emerged out the front door, with Jason in shorts and a tank top, right behind her.

"Oh, how sweet," Glen said, with the binoculars stuck to his head.

They backed out the driveway and drove his way.

Glen slunk down in the seat and thought, *Good thing I'm not in my car*. He started his motor once they passed, swung a U-turn, and followed a safe distance behind. "I'm having so much fun killing you," he reiterated, "And you don't even have a clue."

Block after block, he followed, always leaving at least two, usually three cars between them. Finally, the Jeep Cherokee, his dad's Jeep Cherokee, turned into the Worlds' Gym.

Glen parked as far away as possible and made note, literally, of the time, 2:57 p.m. He waited. Exactly one hour and thirteen minutes later, the two emerged, laughing like they didn't have a worry in the world.

He followed them home but saw no need to hang around.

The next day's surveillance showed no movement of any kind.

The following day at 2:37 p.m., the two emerged.

"Boy, are these two predictable," Glen said, as Gloria and Jason once again, decked in their gear, headed for the gym.

Still not 100% better, particularly when he was in the contaminated house, Glen had no desire for relapse. He drove back to El Cajon's army surplus store, hoping to get some kind of decent chemical suit. "What better place to find one."

His choices seemed limited. The equipment, although more than worthy, was cumbersome, bulky, and just plain outdated, to say the least. He chose an army green, battery-operated one-piece suit with head and face gear attached and a replaceable screw-on canister filter.

"Overkill?" His stomach growled as a sharp pain shot through his head. "I don't think so."

Back at the house, he put on his silly gear and looked at himself in his full-length mirror. "I look like something out of a sci-fi movie," he chuckled. "Some kind of monster." He paused and looked at himself for several minutes, not quite sure why or that he was even doing it. He just stood and stared.

Stumbling with the suit's awkward footwear, he clunked his way to the chemical room with a mason jar and a box of freezer baggies in hand. He hadn't been in this section of the house for any reason since he nearly killed himself so many days before. The bucket sat untouched. The walls, counters, and faucets looked like they were glowing with a red, green, and yellow moss–type substance coming off of them. The wall-to-wall carpet was completely gone, from wall to wall. The door didn't want to open, Glen pushed harder, the hinges protested, and the door reluctantly gave way.

The battery–pack hummed, pumping fresh filtered oxygen into his lungs as he cautiously stepped over the threshold. His head throbbed, pounding to his heartbeat, and shaking he reached for the bucket, that was slightly stuck to the ground. He lifted. It came free, leaving a perfect circle of carpet under it, the only carpet left in the room.

He didn't want to touch it, not even with the thick chemical-resistant gloves that came with the suit. He set the bucket down on the moss-covered counter.

Using the mason jar, he scooped out a bunch of clear shards and vigilantly screwed the lid in place. Snapping open one of the freezer bags, he slipped the jar in it and sealed the bag. He did this three more times, four baggies in all.

"Nothing, no animal or human could be dumb enough to get in this," he told himself, before placing all his gear—the suit, the shoes, gloves, everything on the back porch and raced for the shower.

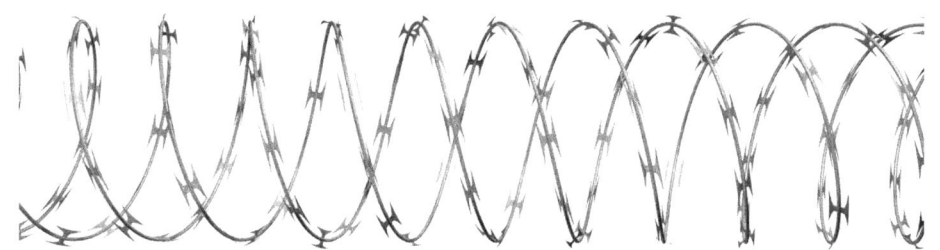

CHAPTER 13

ESCALATING CHAOS

COs could kill someone without a problem, meaning a half-day lockdown, maybe a day, but when an inmate took a life, we were usually locked up a day or two, sometimes more.

Ya see, here's the thing. When we're locked up, the cops have to do all the work, which, believe me, there was a lot of. We're not just talking about feeding us in our cells, which was so much work, needless to mention the meal preparations. Then, cleaning up afterward? Complete chaos. Inmates literally run the joint; the cops are merely babysitters.

I didn't recognize either of the COs that brought us dinner. When I asked how long we were looking at, they gave no reply. Although they did leave our dirty trays sitting in the dayroom, this being an indication we'll probably be out in the morning.

"So… do you have any questions?" Glen asked.

"Not yet, but I probably will."

Intrigued, I continued to read.

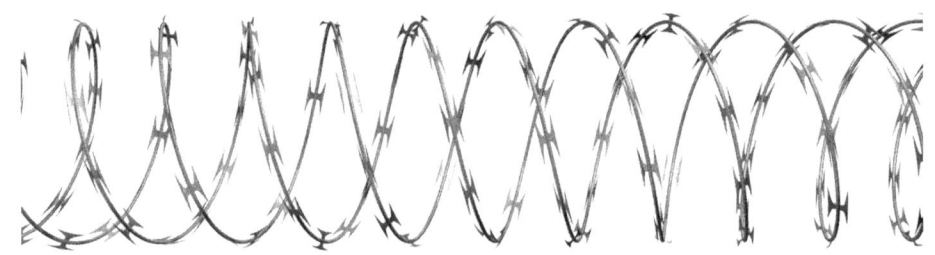

CHAPTER 14

POOR DOG

The following morning the suit was lying in the middle of the yard. As Glen retrieved it, he noticed his next-door neighbor carrying their Labrador retriever to their minivan. Unfortunately, he didn't look too well, with his legs draped toward the ground and his head flopping from side to side.

"Good luck, poor fella," Glen murmured on his way back inside. Was it his paranoia? Guilt perhaps? Either way, he could have sworn his neighbor scowled before driving away.

Tomorrow was Gloria's birthday. Glen figured the family would gather, *perfect— the more, the better*, he thought while inspecting the suit for leaks. Two small surface tears, no holes.

The most disturbing part was the urine. For whatever reason, apparently, the stupid dog peed on it. *No big deal, the gloves and mask should suffice.* Carefully he placed his little pint of hell in the rental's trunk and resumed his stakeout position.

2:30 ... 2:50 ... 3:30, no sign of movement.

Suddenly Gloria emerged, by herself. Jason must have stayed home.

He followed her to the grocery store just because it seemed like the thing to do. She came out of the store twenty-seven minutes later, pushing a shopping cart with at least one cake and what looked like several pies and a couple brown paper sacks. Adding solidity to Glen's suspicions of tomorrow's party.

That night Glen lay talking to himself. "How do you know they will even go to the gym tomorrow?"

"Oh, they'll go alright."

"How do you know?"

"Because everything's just going so right, nothing can go wrong."

He smiled as he floated off to deep sleep.

Even though his body had seemed to stabilize, his mind obviously continued to deteriorate.

Leaving little to no room for error, he started his stakeout at 7:00 a.m. the following morning. "Gloria's special day," he said with a smile on his way to the car. Throughout the day, Gloria left for a short time twice, and Jason left once. Glen was starting to worry.

2:30 ... 2:35, 36, 37, 2:40 ... 2:50? ... 2:58, the front door opened, and the two stepped out, dressed in their workout gear.

"Perfect," Glen said from under the binoculars.

After the two had passed, he started the car and drove straight to his Dad's house. He parked in the driveway, popped the trunk, got out, and grabbed the baggies containing the mason jar. He slid down the side of the garage, hoping his key would still work on the back door. It did.

The distant odor of slow-cooked meat, probably a roast, stimulated his senses, nearly pulling him out of his murderous trance. After a brief doubtful pause, he continued toward the kitchen.

Some months back, Glen had actually installed his father's water purification system. It consisted of one single charcoal-filled canister. Creeping through the quiet house with the only sound coming from his heartbeat and the central air, he was nervous, real nervous, to the point of hallucinating with each crack and shadow harboring some hidden predator waiting to pounce.

Wasting as little time as possible, in spite of his fears, he quickly made his way to the kitchen. Something was cooking in the oven. A crockpot sat steaming on the counter. The aroma was overwhelming, immediately reminding Glen of the long, lonely span since his last home-cooked meal.

He opened the sink cupboard. The filter hung untouched right where he mounted it, with multiple opened and unopened objects, bottles of all shapes and sizes, boxes big and little, all blocking his way. He began neatly placing them across the kitchen floor. This took what felt like forever, knowing to make a mess, to leave a stain or any sign he was there would quite possibly compromise his mission.

In his pocket, he carried a screwdriver, two crescent wrenches, and just to be safe, a pair of vice–grips. He reached up and turned off the water to the filter. Next, he cracked the first nut on the waterline. Water sprayed, splashing him in the face. "No, no," he pleaded as he reached for a hand towel that hung on the cupboard door.

The spray stopped as fast as it started, being mere pressure trapped in the system. He quickly dabbed up the remaining water and broke the other nut. The mounting bracket was secured with two simple screws.

Within minutes he was holding the fourteen-inch object in his hand. He tried to unscrew the top. Wet, the canister spun in his hand. He wrapped it in the moist towel and twisted with all his might. The top slowly turned.

Suddenly, he heard a car. Glen reached for his father's service pistol tucked down the front of his pants and rushed to the window.

"Execute plan B. Shoot them both if they come home."

Luckily, it was only the neighbor across the street who paused looking at Glen's rental before she went in her house.

He hurried back to the kitchen. The filter had leaked, saturating the hand towel, and running two feet across the floor, soaking all the contents he had so neatly placed on the tile.

He ran to the hall closet and grabbed a full-sized bath towel. Minutes later and back on track, he unscrewed the canister's lid and poured out some of its charcoal into the towel. Pressed for time and scared to death, he swiftly put on the gloves and reached for the poison.

He peeled through the baggies, instantly getting to the jar. It seemed to glow. From his seated position, he held it up to the kitchen window. The shards sparkled in the midday sunlight.

Wishing he had his mask and gloves; Glen reluctantly cracked the seal. The little jar, now so big, made a hissing sound as the lid came free. A thick purple, ghost-like mist emanated from the jar. Glen choked. An instant reminder of how close he came to death from these evil little crystals.

He swiftly sprinkled close to half the jar content into the filter and instantly secured the lid. Content with his mission thus far, he reinstalled the system and replaced all the under-sink items, right where he found them, taking painstaking seconds to dry each one.

Glen stood and inspected his area. Nothing looked out of place, no dirt, dust, water, nothing. He even replaced the hand towel with a perfect match from one of the drawers. Before he left, he removed all the ice from the auto ice maker's tray, and hot water rinsed it down the drain. Satisfied, he slipped out the back door.

As he drove away, he noticed a curtain move across the street. "Yeah, keep it up, and you'll be next," he mumbled to himself.

Back at his house, no more than an hour later, after purging the last of his blood-streaked stomach bile, Glen thought, *please. No, not again. I have no time for this. I have to pull it together*.

He laid on the cool marble bathroom tile and stared into space while his stomach finally settled. With his head once again pounding, *Had it ever stopped*? He drug himself to the couch, where he kept a waiting bottle of Tylenol and a glass of water.

After their usual one hour of fitness, Gloria and her baby, thirty-five-year-old Jason, hurried home. They had a big evening ahead. The neighbor lady rushed them the minute they pulled in the driveway.

"Hi Gloria, some man came by. I don't know what he was doing, but he stayed for about thirty minutes."

"What did this man look like?"

"I couldn't get a good look at him, but I think he was tall— Oh," she reached in her apron pocket, "I have his license plate number right here. It was some kind of small grey car, a newer one."

"Hum, maybe he left a note. Thanks, Marge."

They started to walk inside. "Marge, today's my birthday."

"Happy Birthday, I didn't know," Marge whined.

"Why, thank you. Listen, we're having a little get–together tonight. You're more than welcome to stop by, say around 6:00?"

"How nice, maybe I will if it's not too much trouble?"

"No, no trouble at all. 6:00, see you there."

"That was nice of you. What gives?" Jason asked

"Well, ya see, son, it's like this. How old do you think Marge is?"

"I don't know, two, three hundred, give or take."

"And since we've lived here, how many times have you seen someone at her house?"

"Um, never."

"Exactly, so when she dies, which no doubt is coming soon, who do you think she's going to leave her stuff to?"

"I see."

"Boy, sometimes I think you may have been swapped at birth."

"So, who do you think came by?" Jason asked.

"No one came by," Gloria answered. "What I think is Marge is a very lonely, very nosey old lady who should probably get a cat or something. Come on, we've got work to do."

First, Jason made two one-gallon pitchers of tea, which he cooled with ice while Gloria started on the vegetables, all of which had purified water from her lovely tap.

Expected were, of course, Gloria and Jason, two more of her sons, Donny and Charley (the oldest), Donny's fiancé, Marge, the nosey neighbor, and Jason's part-time girlfriend would probably stop by. Ricky, being Safeway's' store manager, had to work.

Seven,—far exceeding Glen's wildest imagination.

With the table set, people began to arrive. Roast beef and glazed baked ham were the main courses, with rice, potatoes, vegetables, water, water, and more water.

Glasses of ice water. Glasses of iced tea. Everything was prepared with water, everything was soaked in water, iced in water. Everything on the table was contaminated with Glen's evil brew, just waiting to strike, waiting to lash–out and destroy, waiting to completely annihilate its' unsuspecting victims.

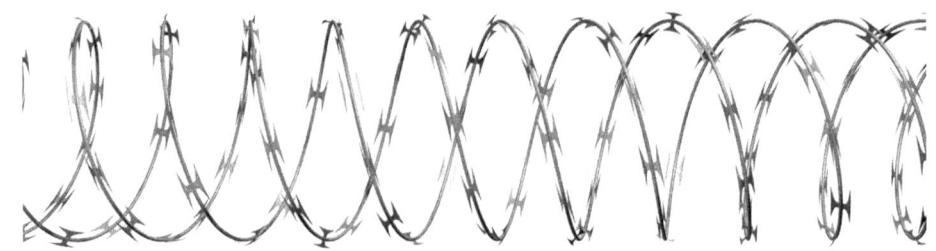

CHAPTER 15

THE CAPTAIN

Not that I was watching it, but my TV signed off. I looked at my clock, 2:48 a.m. I had to get at least a little rest before work. Unlike other three-cent an hour or less jobs, I worked in PIA, Prison Industry Authority. I made a whopping $167.00 per month, primarily sewing prison clothes. You know, like those orange jumpsuits commonly seen on TV and the standard prison-issue blues?

Although, we won't get off the lockdown until the Warden or Captain gets in, tomorrow should be a short day, with possibly no work at all. Regardless, pushing 3:00 a.m., I fell fast asleep.

Seconds after, I heard the central unlock, meaning our doors could now open and close ten minutes on the hour, and people were at my cell.

"Dave, listen, dawg."

"Dave, you got a minute?"

"Dave."

"Dave."

Shit was pissing me off. I got up and headed to the yard.

"Shorty, where's your celly?" I asked.

"He should be out any minute. What's up, dawg?"

"I'll talk to Brian when he gets here."

"Wilson, report to the Lieutenant's office, WILSON– H8357-7, report to Lieutenant Fisher's office," the loud-speaker screeched.

"What the fuck?"

"All part of the job, bro," Shorty said.

"Yeah, a job I don't want."

I waited outside the LT's door for fifteen plus minutes when a CO finally emerged.

"Mr. Wilson, the Captain will see you now."

'The *Captain?'* I thought.

Although seeing the *Warden* was not completely unheard of, a personal meeting with him certainly was ... his Captain, however, was much more accessible. Matter of fact, outside of an occasional drift through the chow hall, I couldn't recall ever laying eyes on the Warden. The Captain, in his early-to-mid-50s was huge, dwarfing the LT's desk.

"Mr. Wilson, have a seat."

By-passing the metal fold-up chairs, no doubt designated for situations just like this, I chose a black leather and wood high back model, sitting in front of his desk. This being the first time in over five years I had sat in anything other than metal or plastic.

The Captain smiled, creasing his basketball-size face, "I'm Captain Cramer."

"Mr. Wilson, I'm a man who pulls no punches. I'm assuming you are as well, or your 'homeboys' wouldn't have placed you in this position."

He looked at the CO who had ushered me in and said, "Could you give us a minute."

"No problem, sir, I'll be right outside."

"Now, Mr. Wilson, as you know, this is a supermax prison. We have some very dangerous, very high-profile people here, to say the least." He got up and poured himself a black cup of coffee.

"As you probably also know, 'Shot callers' are against the rules here." He paused for effect. "However, being I find it impossible to run a prison like this without them, I not only allow it, I encourage it. So, if something comes up—something you feel is getting over your head, out of control, then you let me know, and I'll have the problem on the next bus rolling, and or ten feet in the ground. Do you follow me?" He took a drink of his coffee.

"With all due respect, sir, this isn't a job for me. I'm going home soon."

"Not if I say you're not, you aren't."

"I realize that, sir, as I was saying, someone will be filling this position ASAP. I'm just passing through."

"Like who?"

"Well, sir, ya see that's the thing, we're not sure right now. But believe me, I'm not the one."

"So, you're one of the problems I mentioned?"

"Absolutely not, sir. Like I said, I'm trying to go home, is all."

"Well, your friend Pac-man, I believe is his name, may not be back for some time. As it turns out, his spine was damaged. They're not sure if he will walk again."

"I'm sorry to hear that, sir."

"Yeah, I'm told you two were friends."

"Old cellys, actually, sir."

"I see. Well, Mr. Wilson, you guys get your shit together, and as soon as you do, let me know."

"We will, sir. May I go now?"

The Captain paused as if he was contemplating the question.

"Yes, you may. Send my officer in on your way out, Mr. Wilson."

"Thank you, sir."

Brian was waiting when I got back to the yard.

"Dave, listen bro."

"No, you listen. We're voting today, and I'm not on the roster. This shit is way too much stress for me. As our leader, I'm organizing a vote today. Hear me, Bri?"

Brian laughed, "Yeah, I hear you, dawg. I got it."

"I just learned we may never see Pac-man again. They think he's paralyzed."

"Who said that?"

"The fuckin' Captain dude. I got the Captain yelling at me. I'm telling ya, Bri, I don't like this shit!"

"I get it, Dave, now on a more serious note, the homies want to hit Kevin today. They're waiting for your reply."

"Hit him. I don't give a fuck!" Kill this whole motherfuckin' yard. I DON'T CARE!—Brian, I just want to go home, bro, you know what I'm saying?"

Brian looked over and nodded to a group of people who gathered near bye.

A scared, stone-faced youngster stepped out and rushed across the yard.

I started walking towards my building when shots rang out.

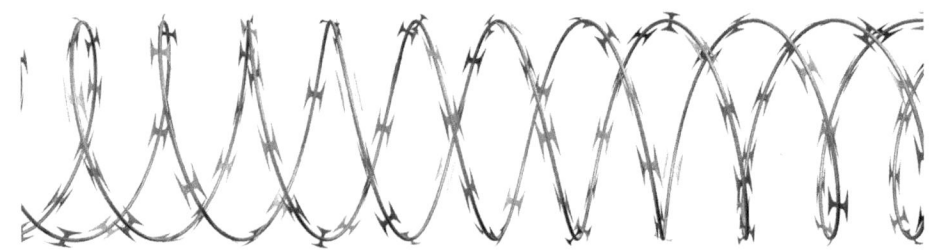

CHAPTER 16

GRADUAL INSANITY

"Happy birthday to you, happy birthday to you, happy birthday, dear Gloria." The song went on.

"Thank you, thank you. Let's eat."

First, Donny's ninety-eight-pound fiance developed a scratchy throat. It seemed so harmless as she gulped water, followed by iced tea.

Soon to follow was Marge, the neighbor.

In mere minutes everyone began to choke.

Gloria stood up, holding her throat. She tried to walk, her legs refused to cooperate, buckling at the knees, she hit the ground.

Marge fell face-first right in her meal.

Everyone lost all motor skills. Their hands fell to their sides, their middles hinged, some hit the ground, others fell forward. Soon, no one could even cough, as their lungs filled with the blood that flowed from their noses and mouths.

The last to die was the birthday girl who helplessly lay completely paralyzed and stared at the phone a mere fifteen feet away.

Curious, Glen was mesmerized when he saw the number of vehicles lining the front yard while conducting a simple drive-by. *Oh boy,— this is gonna be a mess.* Little did he know.

The following morning, after returning the rental, Glen wasn't surprised when he saw the cars untouched and still in place.

He parked a couple houses away, being the closest spot left, and slipped around the back.

No curtain moved from across the street today.

He knocked on the door. Nothing.

After cracking the door a few inches, he hollered, "Hello?"— still no reply.

Glen slowly stepped inside, "Hel..." he choked as an acidic rancid odor sapped the air from his lungs. He raised his shirt over his mouth and nose and groaned, "Hello, is anybody home?" As he cautiously crept down the hall.

Nothing, absolutely nothing, could prepare him for the mayhem, the madness, the complete chaotic insanity that lay before him.

So many people, "Where did they all come from?" All dead. He didn't need to check.

Dried blood crusted their faces. Their eyes looked like little blood Jello cups. Their throats boiled, blistered, and burnt away, exposing cartilage and bone. Their limbs laid undisturbed like they had simply fallen asleep. But Glen, through experience, knew better.

He could barely identify even the most familiar faces.

Gloria laid shriveled and decayed, with her head awkwardly twisted to the side.

A male, Glen assumed to be Jason, sat upright at the table, like some kind of statue. Missing were his nose, eyes, and lips, leaving only his teeth and forehead, which freakishly appeared undisturbed.

Donny, Glen recognized from his uptight attire, also sat upright with his facial features similarly burnt away.

An old lady laid face forward with vertebrae's protruding from her neck. Aside from a small female, who was possibly Donny's fiancé, Glen didn't or couldn't distinguish any of the remaining three bodies.

Seven people. "Aren't you guys a mess?" He chuckled. "Hey Gloria, how you feeling? You still want me to move?"

"Jason, you little prick, what are you smiling about?" Glen laughed.

"Donny, you've been served—I've always wanted to say that!"

Glen laughed like the lunatic he had become as he pushed Charley from his chair and took a seat at the head of the table. Placing his hands in front of his face, he began to pray.

"Dear Lord, bless this food." He roared with hysterical laughter.

Living in a delusional world, Glen had yet to consider the consequence for what he had done. Thinking, *I'll stay here, get rid of the bodies, take back all my properties, sell them and relocate ... somewhere, maybe Hawaii, or Alaska or maybe I'll just stay right here.*

He tried to pick up one of the females. Her decomposing body came apart in his hands.

In the tool shed out back, he located some shovels and a wheelbarrow. Leaving the bodies where they laid, he started to dig, drawing the unwanted attention of at least one neighbor from an upstairs window.

The ground was hard-packed, and with no more than twelve inches complete, being out of shape, he began to tire, his hands already blistering. "This isn't going to work."

Glen looked up and once again saw the nosey neighbor standing in their window.

"A backhoe, I'm gonna need a backhoe." He covered up his little hole, placed the shovels back in the shed, and parked the wheelbarrow right outside the back door.

Paranoid, he felt like people everywhere were watching him, all the way to the rental company.

"Too big, it's just too big. I can't even see a way to get it in the backyard." He said to himself, drawing the observation of the service attendant.

"Can I help you, sir?"

"No, I don't believe so. It's just too big."

Driving away, racked for ideas, Glen said, "A Mexican, I need a Mexican or several."

He drove to Home Depot, where he had seen early morning migrant workers seeking under–the–table employment. He'd never paid much attention to them, never really thought about what they were doing out there lined up on the side of the parking lot.

While he sat observing the situation, an older red Ford pickup truck stopped and quickly scooped up four of the five men standing in line. Glen, with his long skinny, shaved head and yellowed black eyes, rushed over and rolled down his passenger window, startling the little Mexican, who stepped back on the curb.

"You work?" Glen barked.

The Mexican looked around, hoping to find some other alternative, anything, other than this obviously crazy white man. With limited early afternoon choices, the Mexican reluctantly stepped forward.

"Si, I work."

"Get in."

The two drove away.

"I need you to dig a hole or holes. I need you to dig some holes. Can you dig holes?"

"Si, I dig hole."

Glen had his doubts. The Mexican couldn't have been more than five and a half feet tall and probably weighed less than a buck forty.

"I need several, a few?" Glen held up some fingers, "Ten feet deep holes. Do you understand?"

Being an illegal alien fresh from Mexico, he knew all too well the meaning of a 'ten-foot hole.' Scared, the Mexican sat and stared.

"Do you understand?"

"Si, I work." The little Mexican chirped in broken English.

With no more than bottled water to fuel him, the Mexican chopped, hacked, pounded, and shoveled the hard earth for the next three and a half hours, making little progress.

The sun was setting. Glen measured the first and only hole. "forty-two inches, just over three feet, a yard, one yard."

A camera flash from the neighbor's window caught both Glen's and the Mexican's eyes.

"Okay, let's call it a day. How 'bout I pick you and some of your friends up tomorrow morning?"

The Mexican glanced back at the window, then at Glen. He paused and said, "Si."

After paying him $50, which Glen felt to be generous for less than four hours of work, he dropped him back at Home Depot.

It was dark when Glen got home.

Several more camera flashes lit up his yard as he awkwardly muscled the wheelbarrow through the back door.

Once inside, he stopped to catch his breath, peeking out the back window curtain as he did.

"Honey, I think that might be the man Gloria told us about, the one she had to get the restraining order against." The neighbor said as she stared through the binoculars with her camera in hand.

"Stop being so damn nosey, Evelyn!" Her husband barked from his lazy–boy recliner.

Evelyn continued her relentless surveillance well into the evening.

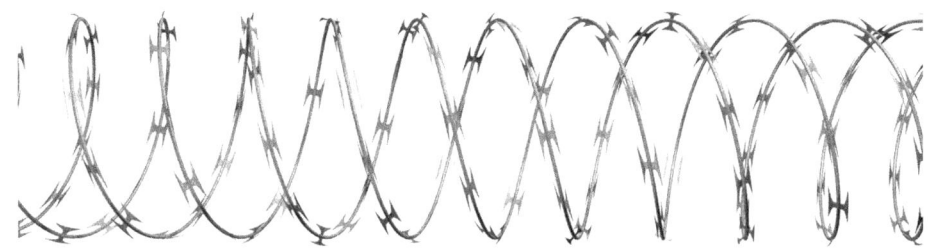

CHAPTER 17

THE GOLDEN GLOVE BOXER

One of, if not the most unfortunate thing about being on lockdown, for me, was no cinnamon rolls. Basically, because there were no inmates to bake them. Truth be known, all the food during lockdown sucked for this exact reason. Plus, after years of watching inmates spit in guards' food, how could I be comfortable eating meals prepared by guards for us?

About the only thing you could rely on a CO doing right was the mail, and half the time, he fumbled that too. Something I found great humor in was the famous letter–switch. Commonly, when a guard would find an inmate love–lettering someone other than his wife, he would switch the letters. Try explaining that to the old lady?

Some COs were just there to do their eight hours and be gone. Others, however, felt it their solemn duty to torture us any and every way they could.

We returned this favor whenever the opportunity arose. On one such occasion, a celly of mine worked in the CO lounge. Stupid thing letting an inmate work in the guard's lounge.

Anyway, every Wednesday, he prepared this "special burger" for a guard named Landers. On a regular basis, you could hear Landers ranting and raving about how good his burger was. "I'm telling you— this kid makes the best burger this side of the Mississippi," the big corn-fed redneck would bellow.

One late night my celly, Jim was his name, said, "Have you ever wondered what's so damn special about that cop's magic burgers?"

"Afraid to ask," I chuckled.

"I don't blame ya. Anyway, I unscrewed the drain, the one right in the middle of the floor, and every Wednesday, I rub his raw meat patty around the lip like it was a fuckin' rag, then I fry it, hair, and all, sometimes I spit on it too." Jim laughed like this was the funniest thing he had ever said in his life, and quite frankly, it probably was.

"Dave," a soft male voice whispered into my cell.

"Yeah, Angel," I addressed the six feet four-inch homosexual standing at my door. Angel was an ex Golden Glove boxer who had been taking female hormones for the past few years in hopes of one day becoming the woman he felt himself to be.

On long-term lockdowns, which apparently this had become, the guards let the homosexuals out to do the running. Things like getting us hot water, dropping letters in the outbox, and in some cases, delivering contraband from cell to cell. Why? I don't know. It's just how California State prison ran in the '90s.

"You guys need anything in there?" Angel asked.

"No, we're good. How long we gonna be down?"

"Rumor has it, one week. Apparently, the Warden is tired of the bullshit. Seems like someone's been getting shot once to twice a week lately."

"Yeah, I know. Thanks, Angel."

I first met Angel three years back, during a raid, when a CO found and destroyed a houseplant I had. I loved that plant, had it a couple years. During the aftermath, in which of course, the homosexuals were cleaning up, Angel came to my door.

"Excuse me."

I looked up from my book and ignored him.

"Excuse me, Dave, is it?"

"Yeah, what's goin' on?" I walked to the door.

"Hi, I'm Angel. I thought you might want this?"

I looked toward the top of the door, to the crack, where Angel was holding a clipping from my plant. I reached for it and stopped.

"Listen, Angel, was it? I'm not into nothing funny, ya know what I'm saying?"

"Take the damn thing."

I accepted the gift.

"Look, Dave, I've been watching how you conduct yourself and how people treat you."

"And?"

"And I'm not involved, 'like that' with several of my friends. So, if you wanted to be friends, I'm okay with it."

Homosexuals didn't only run things during lockdown. They ran shit all the time. The weed, alcohol, smokes, drugs, ink, everything somewhere had a queer behind it. If you didn't have at least one on the team, you were lagging, and lagging was no way to be in prison.

For the next few days, I read page after page of doctors' opinions on Glen's sanity, or lack thereof. Of course, the prosecutor wanted the death penalty. Therefore, he had to prove Glen was sane at the time of the murders. So, any and all shrinks hired by him declared Glen sane.

Unfortunately for the prosecutor, all other doctors swore him to be the raving lunatic he obviously was. I'll write more on that later. For now, let's get back to the story.

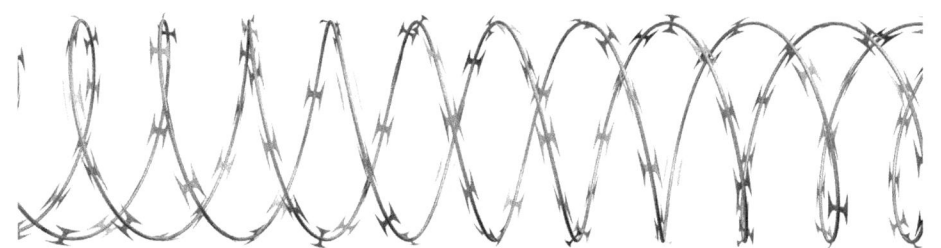

CHAPTER 18

MEXICO

S craping both walls, the wheelbarrow barely squeezed down the hall. Once free of this cumbersome task, Glen began collecting wallets, purses, car keys, pocket change, and jewelry. $16.00, $23.00, and $56.00, four wristwatches, and some cheap jewelry in all. Most victims had soiled themselves, making this process a little more difficult than it should have been.

"Yes, the cars, what to do with them? Four cars. Well, I obviously can't bury them.

Mexico, that's it! I'll drive them south and sell 'um cheap."

Early–kill flies swarmed when Glen tried to lift the smallest body into the wheelbarrow, missing the bucket's center, the barrow fell to the side, spilling its content back to the floor.

Wheeling, he tried again. The wheelbarrow dumped to the other side. He lost his balance and fell, landing face-first into the wall.

"You think this is funny, Jason?" He barked as he drug his sore body off the ground.

Angry, he yanked the body up and successfully slammed it in place.

"You're next, you little prick," he said to Jason as he wheeled past.

Twelve wooden stairs led to the basement. When Glen was a kid, he used to go down there to read, study, tinker with Dad's tools, build model planes, whatever. Comfortable with this environment, he went down to check it out. A couple of mattresses and an old couch were shoved up against the walls. Dad's workbench, although missing a few of the pegboard-placed tools, looked basically undisturbed. Glen headed up the stairs to the waiting wheelbarrow.

Once comfortably stabilized with both hands firmly in place, he lifted the barrow. The body slid out like liquid, seeping over a waterfall, and tumbled down the stairs, striking the bottom like a sack of rocks.

"You know Jason, I'm starting to see you in a different light. I mean, you're always smiling," Glen said as he wheeled back into the room. "You're always spreading good cheer. Maybe I had you wrong."

Jason's skinless face sat and stared through empty eye sockets, grinning with blood-strained, pearly-white teeth.

Glen walked over and pulled a glass from the cupboard. "I think I might even be starting to enjoy your company."

He filled the glass with water. "Yeah." Glen raised the glass towards his mouth. "Maybe I'll send you downstairs last?"

He placed his lips to the glass. Suddenly, he dropped it. It shattered in the sink.

"Thought you were going to trick me, didn't you?" Glen laughed. "Ya almost got me. Not this time, though. No, not this time."

He went back down the stairs and came back with the tools to remove the deadly water filter. "I'll just cap the line until I can replace the filter. What do you think, Jason, you good with that?"

Glen waited for a reply.

"Okay, be that way. I'm gonna take your silence as agreement, though."

After capping the line, he carefully placed the filter in several black trash bags, then emptied the refrigerator's automatic ice bucket in the sink. Exhausted with his efforts thus far, he decided to drive the first car to Tijuana, a mere twelve miles away.

"Hey, Jason, you wanna go for a ride?" He chose Donny's dark blue BMW.

"I've always wanted to drive one of these," he said to himself as he left the curb, adjusting the radio. Failing to find opera, he settled for a classical station, one to relax his body for the short twenty-three-minute drive. Jason stayed behind.

Going into Mexico wasn't a problem; there was never a line. Now getting out, on the other hand, being a two-to-four-hour ordeal, was a complete nightmare.

Leaving the calm, clean, organized America behind, Glen found himself lost in a world of hurling mayhem, with cars and people everywhere, all doing something. What?

With no clue where to go and no plan in place, he pulled into the first parking lot he found. A light rain began to fall, glazing the formerly filthy vehicles to a glistening sheen. No people were in sight. Glen eased the Beemer through the muddy lot and slowly approached a little white shack sitting off to the side.

A skinny Mexican stepped out. Glen cracked his window, "You buy?

The Mexican walked around the car as if to inspect it.

"$500," Glen said.

The Mexican paused skeptically.

"You buy $500," Glen repeated himself.

The Mexican came to the window. "$200."

Glen had hoped for more but was in no position to barter.

$200, okay. I bring three, tres more."

The Mexican was quick to pay; after all, this was his lucky day.

Glen walked back to the port of entry and stood in line for the next three hours.

70

Finally reaching the booth, the agent, startled by Glen's beat-up desolate appearance, asked, "What happened to you?"

Before Glen could answer, the man said, "Could you please step into secondary for me sir, thank you. Next."

"Identification, please." The black lady demanded.

Glen reached for his wallet, which wasn't there.

"I don't have any"

"What do you mean, you don't have any?"

"Jason has it."

"What, Who's Jason?"

"I left it at home."

"You're confusing me. What's your name?" Her fingers hit the keyboard. "Come on, quit wasting my time. Name?"

"Sombers, Glen Sombers."

He went on to give his Social Security number and address.

Being none of his story added up as to what exactly he was doing in their beautiful city, he was held and questioned for another two hours.

After hailing a cab, he got back to his Dad's around midnight. Spent, he laid on the couch, just feet from the massacre.

"Good night, Jason, Oh, and I'm gonna need my wallet back," Glen bellowed before rolling over and falling fast asleep.

"Mom, Jason, is anybody home?" Someone yelled.

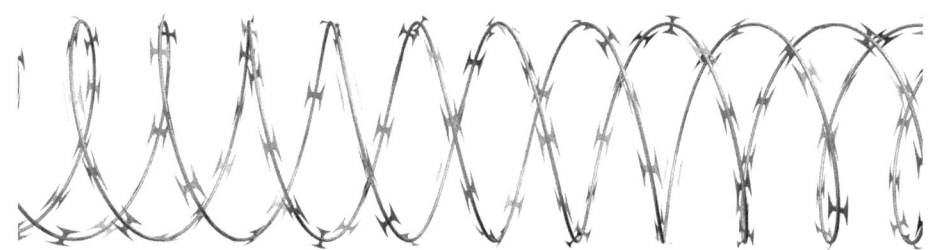

CHAPTER 19

INMATES DROPPING LIKE FLIES!

After five days, with the door only opening once for a quick ten-minute shower, that in reality was probably no more than seven, the little six-by-ten foot cell was getting cramped. Granted, neither I, nor Glen were rookies to the lockdown situation. Regardless, it still became a little monotonous at times.

"I have a backgammon game," Glen said one night after chow.

"Shoot it."

That became our new thing. Hour after hour, we played that stupid game. If there were professional backgammon competitions, we would have been pros of the pros.

Glen's square ass grew on me. He didn't radiate with personality, as I think most squares don't, but he was pleasant and occasionally verging on funny. Like when he would pull the "look over there," pointing out the long vertical window, while he swiped a cookie off my lunch tray or moved one of his game pieces.

I could always tell when he had done something by the silly grin he was trying so desperately to hide. On the morning of day seven, mine and three other doors popped.

"Wilson, Montgomery, Lopez, and Chan … report to the Lieutenant's office."

Filthy and unshaven, I uncomfortably drug myself, with a caravan of reps, one from each race, down the stairs and across the yard to the LT's office. The Captain was leaning against the desk when we got there.

"Gentlemen, what the hell's going on?"

This was actually a good question, one for which I nor any of the other reps had an answer. Heroin? No, it was always there. Literally, nothing had changed. But for some reason, we had gone from one to two casualties every two or three months to five or six a month. Whether they were shot or stabbed, people were dropping like flies.

I spoke up, "Sir, we're no more sure than you are."

"Fair enough. Spread the word I want things the way they used to be. If I don't get what I want, we're going to start six to twelve–month lockdowns. Am I making myself clear?"

"Yes, sir." We all chirped in unison.

"You guys will come off lockdown today."

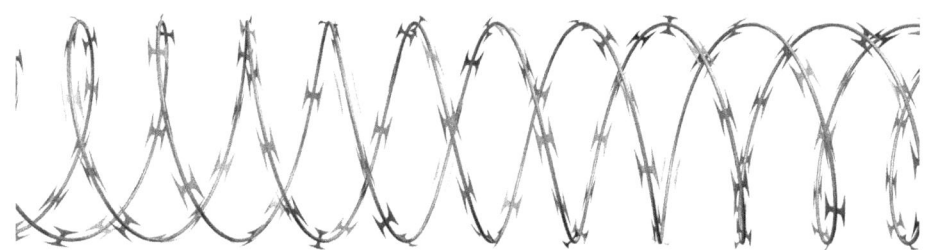

CHAPTER 20

RICKY'S DEMISE

Glen flew off the couch like he'd been struck by lightning, with his long skinny legs pumping air before they touched the ground. He shot for an adjoining bedroom and clung to the wall.

"Ouch… ouch," Ricky coughed. "Mom, anybody home? What the hell's that smell?" He continued through the foyer.

Glen quietly slipped through the bedroom.

As Ricky moved, Glen moved, keeping at least one wall between them.

"What the hell. Mom? Jason?"

Ricky headed to his mother's bedroom across the house.

Glen had left his pistol on the workbench downstairs. With no time to get it, quickly, he snuck to the kitchen and grabbed a large butcher knife from the cutlery block. He looked at Jason and raised a finger to his lips, indicating for the corpse to remain quiet.

"Mom?"

Ricky had yet to reach the kitchen. Glen carefully circled him, ready to strike with the knife.

"Jason!" He continued to yell through the lifeless house.

Suddenly, Ricky's blood–curdling scream echoed through the house, shook the walls and could be heard down the entire block.

Crazed with psychotic rage, Glen, screaming even louder than his soon-to-be-victim, jumped into the room slashing the knife back and forth in front of him, and tripped over one of the bodies. Down he went.

Ricky bolted for the front door screaming all the way. Glen found traction and raced after him, also screaming. He wasn't sure why he was yelling, or for that matter, that he was, but yell, he did—all the way down the hall.

Early morning light shot across the carpet as Ricky rushed out the door and ran for his life. With the knife held high, Glen dove off the six-foot porch like an Olympic cliff jumper and brought the blade down in the top of Ricky's head, instantly silencing him. Scraping his right knee and knuckles on the concrete walk, he rode Ricky's twitching body to the bitter end.

Glen jumped up, grabbed his newest victim by the ankles, bouncing his lifeless head across each of the four porch steps. He drug Ricky's body back inside, leaving a trail of blood the whole way. Mentally, physically and emotionally exhausted, Glen gave one final tug as he fell to a sitting position. Panting, he kicked the door shut and laid on the ground, where he stayed for several minutes.

Recovering, he drug himself to a nearby window to basically assess the damages. Everything looked calm. He glanced at a nearby clock. 7:42 a.m.

"Jason, I got you some company."

"Guess."

"No, you guess."

"It's your brother, Dummy. How could you not know that?"

Glen looked back out the window. "Looks like I have another car to deal with. What is that thing Ricky, some kind of Toyota, Honda or something?"

"Oh, now you're gonna give me the silent treatment too, huh? Okay, I can deal with that. But don't think you're going to sit up here with me and Jason. No sir, you're going downstairs, buddy boy!"

First, before the neighborhood began to stir, he made a soapy solution in a bucket. Using a push–broom and a water–hose, he washed the blood trail away. Next, he grabbed his gun off the workbench, being careful not to trip on the body at the bottom of the stairs, while he swatted at flies with one hand and held his nose with the other. Being day three, the bodies were indeed starting to ripen.

He worked Ricky into the wheelbarrow. "No, Jason, I don't need any help here. You just sit there and smile while I do all the work." Glen paused, actually waiting for Jason to offer a hand. "Wow, ... whatever."

He wheeled the corpse across the house and tumbled the second body down the stairs. "I'm on a roll."

He tried to lift Gloria. Rigor mortis made the process cumbersome, to say the least. After a couple of tries, Gloria, too, tumbled to the depths.

Next would be Donny, who laid on his side as if sound asleep. Glen rolled him over and gasped, "Oh my, what in the world happened to your face?" Similar to his brother Jason, Donny's entire face from the forehead down was missing.

After forty minutes of struggling, Glen finally got Donny secured and down the stairs. Fatigued, he stood on wobbly legs and stared down the basement. All three bodies looked comical, stacked on top of each other, with heads, arms, and legs poking every which way. Glen chuckled.

Pushing noon, he decided to get rid of another car or two. For lack of a better idea, Mexico it would have to be. He checked out Gloria's Chrysler. "No, it looks pretty good sitting there in the driveway. How 'bout this Ford Mustang. Whose is it anyway? I think I may have got these keys from … Donny's fiancé? Who cares? The Mustang it will be."

After cleaning the foyer, Glen left for Mexico. The sun had barely set.

Passing some of his old haunts, like the local baseball field he used to play little league at, with his father always cheering from the sidelines, Glen stared at them but didn't recognize anything. It all looked so foreign, distant, and out of place. His memories felt like possible residue from a book he read or maybe a movie he saw on TV.

His school, one he could never forget, was a distant past. *"Was I ever there, did I ever do that? What's wrong with me?"* Glen thought as he maneuvered the Mustang through Point Loma.

"Awe." He yelled when he looked in his rearview mirror. "I told you to stay home, Jason." Glen spun around and found an empty back seat. "What's wrong with me?"

The Mustang's V8 roared as he shifted into third gear, accelerated, caught fourth, and joined into the early evening flow of traffic headed south down I-5.

As usual, he entered Mexico with ease. Once again, a light rain, sprinkle for say, started to fall. Strange how it's dry in San Diego, yet Tijuana, minutes away, always seemed to have a drizzle?

He pulled into the same dirt mud parking lot. No one came out of the booth. Glen tapped his horn lightly and looked to the front, back, and sides. Eventually, his stepbrother's blue BMW pulled in behind him.

Three Mexicans climbed out. Glen recognized the one he had previously done business with. The other two, both being huge, were strangers to him.

"Senior, you wish to do business?" The six foot-three inch, wide-as-a-building driver asked.

"I do."

"How many cars you have?"

"This one and at least three more."

"All like these two?"

"Yes"

"Okay, here is what we'll do. You bring them to Jack-in-the-Box in San Ysidro, the one right before the border. We'll have someone pick them up there."

"So, I don't have to cross the border?"

"You bring the last one here. I'll pay you."

77

"When?" Glen asked.

"Now. You go get them, and we'll be waiting for you."

"At the Jack-in-the-Box?"

"Yes. We'll take this one now, and you go get the others."

"Okay." Glen stood awkwardly.

"You go."

Glen left on foot and walked once again to the border.

Today's line wasn't too bad. One hour and ten minutes later, Glen was back on American soil, hailing a cab.

'Did I misunderstand something? Why didn't he pay me?' He thought in the short cab ride back to the house.

"Can you meet me at Jack-in-the-Box in like thirty minutes? He asked the driver.

"No problem."

Twenty-six minutes later, he pulled Ricky's Honda into the fast-food parking lot.

The cab was already waiting.

Glen didn't spot anyone who looked familiar or suspect in any way.

He stepped out of the car.

In one fluid motion a Mexican, who appeared out of nowhere, slipped into the driver's seat. He tried to push Glen out of the way, so he could close the door.

"Money," Glen protested.

The Mexican said several things in Spanish, none of which Glen understood.

Reluctantly, Glen got out of the way. The Honda peeled out just as the cab took its place.

Startled and confused, he climbed into the cab and quickly vanished out of the parking lot.

This was all happening a little faster than Glen could think. But the bottom line was the vehicles he so desperately needed to get rid of were quickly disappearing.

In the next hour and a half, he got rid of Charley's Mercedes and Jason's girlfriend's Jeep Wrangler. The only one left was Jason's Chevy Silverado truck. Unfortunately, he would have to drive this one over the border.

"Jason buddy, I know you're not going to like this, but your truck has to go."

"Why?" Glen asked.

"Well, for one, I have nowhere to park it, and for two, I can't afford the insurance. Now, if you want to pay the insurance …?" Glen waited.

"Yeah, that's what I thought. Anyway, it's got to go, buddy boy."

A sure sign of Glen's insanity. Here he was a serial murderer, a monster of the highest degree, and he was concerned about insurance?

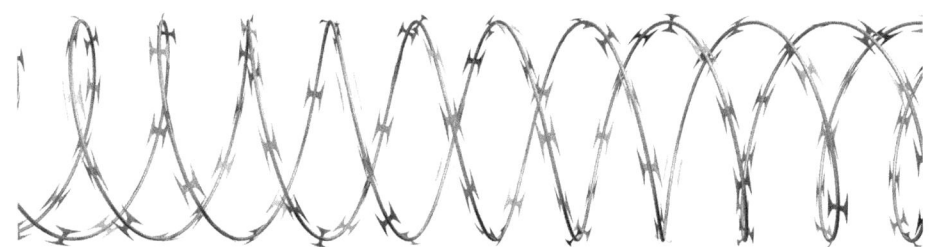

CHAPTER 21

THE GUARDS' FAILURE TO PROTECT

After breakfast in bed, our cell doors opened for the first time in over a week. "Dave, hey bro, you got a minute?" A youngster no more than twenty, named Billy, from northern California asked.

Serving a short two-year term, Billy was a level one inmate who, by way of attempted suicides, each one carrying a few points, had made himself a level four and my neighbor, right next door. He had no homeboys on the yard and little to no protection.

Eager to get outside, Glen stepped around me and was gone.

"What's up, Billy?"

"Listen, Dave, that fuckin' weirdo I live with, he's been paying me $60 a week to put my boxers on backwards and spank myself with this wooden brush."

"What?"

"I know. Anyway, last night …

"… Wait, how long has this been going on?"

"Like … a few months."

"What the fuck, Billy. Why didn't you say something sooner?"

"I needed the money, is all."

"So, why are you coming to me?"

"Well, because last night, I made the horrible mistake of telling Big Red."

"Why would you do that?"

"I don't know. Anyway, Red told some others, and now SFV and IE want me to kill him."

"What the fuck does Inland Empire or SFV got to do with you?"

"I …," Billy whined …

"Look, Billy, this is bad, way bad. Let me go out on the next unlock and see what I can learn. Meanwhile, you lay low."

I wanted to avoid Kirk's stupid ass as much as possible, so I went to Tiny, the IE Rep.

"Tiny, what's up, dawg?"

"All good, all good, what can I help you with, Dave?" Tiny asked while he sat in the shade with his hands behind his head.

"Can we take a walk?"

I found it better to get people away from their homeboys before asking any questions, or better yet, favors. "Listen Tiny, Billy, that dip–shit neighbor of mine, seems to have a little issue with you guys. Do you mind if I ask why?"

"How is this your concern? I mean, he's not from Dago, and it would appear you have your hands full with your own homeboys."

"That's for sure. No, the kid has just kinda grown on me. And I don't quite see why IE or SFV have interest in him."

"Really? Well, I don't know about SFV, but a few months back, he asked for our protection."

"I'm sorry, I did not know that. Tiny, you have a nice day."

"No problem, Dave, and you have a nice day as well."

Pissed off, I walked a couple laps, waiting for the next unlock.

"Why didn't that little fucker tell me that. Maybe save me a little embarrassment?" I asked myself before half the Dago car rushed me with the usual daily harassments.

"Dave, so and so this, so and so that."

"Dave."

"Dave."

"Dave."

"Cut him off."

"Cut him off.'"

"Roll him up."

And every now and then, "Send him my way. We need to talk."

Unlock couldn't have come soon enough. The way it was right now, I didn't even like the yard anymore.

"We're meeting by the bleachers after chow, the whole Dago car, spread the word," I told Shorty.

Billy was waiting when I got back inside.

"So, what happened?"

"Why didn't you tell me you were rolling IE?"

"I don't know Dave; I've never done any of this before."

"Man, shut the fuck up, 'I've never done this before'—are you serious?"

"I know. Look, Dave … I …"

"You, my ass! Don't you think I have enough on my plate already, Billy?"

"I know, but—"

"But nothing, dude. Listen, Billy, I'm trying to help you, and you send me out blind like that? Not cool, not cool at all."

Billy looked at the ground as he shuffled his feet in shame.

"And SFV, what's up with them?"

"I … I thought they ran with IE?"

"Billy, I don't know how you've lived this long. How old are you… eighteen, nineteen?"

"I'm twenty."

"When are you due for release?"

"I'm not sure, but hopefully sometime towards the end of this year, if nothing else happens."

Unable to kick this poor kid to the curb, I looked at him with compassion in my heart and said, "Okay, listen close. First and foremost, put in for a cell change. Second, hang low and see how this thing pans out. But no matter what, you won't be doing weird shit for your freak of a celly no more. Do you hear me?"

The doors popped for the final unlock, a.k.a. yard recall, for the lunch meal.

I was a little surprised we had now made it one-half of the day without an incident. Maybe the Warden's threat of a one-year lockdown had some effect?

Glen came moseying in wearing his shorts, tank top, and running shoes with his headphones in place, basically looking like he didn't have a worry in the world. This lifer–behavior being the exact reason I moved him in.

"What's going on?" He asked.

I stood and chuckled.

"Nothing, my friend. Not a damn thing you should worry about anyway."

He crawled up on his rack, laid back, and started reading a book.

Suddenly a solar eclipse shadowed my door.

"Billy?"

The 420-pound monster, Tiny, whispered through Billy's cell door.

Before Billy replied, the sound of metal bounced on the ground as Tiny kicked a piece of eight-inch sharpened rebar under Billy's door.

"After dinner," he said as he waddled away.

Billy's celly was a large pedophile–looking thirty-six-year-old, overweight white guy who worked as the cops' clerk, which kept him out of the cell most the day.

"Dave," Billy whispered.

"Yeah," I reluctantly answered.

Billy paused, "Did, did you see Tiny?"

"I did."

"Did you hear what he said?"

"I did."

"What, what should I do?"

"Well, Billy, here's the thing, your choices at this point seem incredibly limited. Either you can die, or you can be a lifer."

"What should—what should I do?"

"Listen, Billy, I've never told anyone this before in my life, and hopefully, I will never have to tell anyone it again." I glanced up at Glen, who never took his nose out of his book. "You're going to have to hit the button."

"What?"

"You have to go into protective custody. Believe me, Billy, telling someone to PC up is against everything I stand for, everything I believe in."

"How, how do I do it?"

"I'm not exactly sure, but I'm pretty sure you have to tell the guard you're in fear for your life."

"That's it?"

"I think so."

The doors popped for lunch.

Not wanting to be associated with Billy, I stalled in my cell until he left for the chow hall.

The building was a giant triangle that housed 250 inmates in 125 cells. It had a large two-story structure in its middle, with a CO's office on the bottom and three-armed COs on the top. The upper section was all glass, with gun slots for the COs to shoot out of.

When Glen and I stepped onto the tier, Billy was already in the cop's office. We both already knew what he was doing. So, we casually passed and went to chow.

As we came out of the chow-hall, we saw Billy being escorted to the Lieutenant's office.

Thirty minutes later, while I waited for the next unlock, Billy returned.

"Dave," he whispered across the doors.

"What's up?" I asked.

"Dude, the Lieutenant said, tonight when I go to chow, to not tuck my shirt in, and when the guard hollers at me, to ignore him. Then when they bring me to him, he will lock me up for a few weeks."

Failing to see how this would help, I skeptically asked, "And?"

"He said he knows the exact trouble-makers who are doing this. And, he has them all on the bus in the next week or so. When I get back, they'll be gone."

"Wow, okay. So, tonight you're doing this?"

"Yeah, that's what he said."

The doors opened, and off to the meeting, I went.

About thirty homeboys had already gathered. As I approached, an argument broke out between Shorty and a tall thin guy named Moose, of all people. I mean, here you have Shorty, who couldn't be a centimeter over five-feet three-inches, then ya have Moose, who's well … a moose, towering over our entire car, somewhere around seven feet tall. Moose, the hothead that he was, had just called Shorty a punk ass bitch. This is a major no-no in prison.

Even worse was to have a fight break out between homeboys during a meeting! All bad. We held them back, with Shorty being the hardest to restrain. Go figure.

"Stop! Both of you. Look at the towers right now!" I yelled.

Everyone glanced around the yard at the eleven locked and loaded guns, all pointing at us.

Shorty and Moose just didn't get along. Probably something to do with the atmosphere differences. I don't know. Weird thing was, they knew each other from the streets. I guess they didn't like each other out there, either.

Moose was mine and several other people's choice for rep. To this day, I can't see why anyone would want that job, but hey, power to them.

"Listen, you girls are going to have to slap this shit out later. But for now, I vote for Moose."

Shorty glared.

Moose won the vote by a landslide.

Unfortunately for Moose, on the way back to their building, Shorty jumped him in the sally port. With limited area to move, Moose got stabbed a total of twenty-seven times and lived.

To this day, I'm not quite sure how a man can be stabbed twenty-seven times and live—much less in a sally port under the watchful eyes of not one, but two armed guards with no one seeing a thing. (Although, I did kill a moose once in Alaska. Shot that beast nine times with a twelve-gauge, stuck four, double ought, buck and five magnum slugs in him from twenty feet away. We tracked that moose for over a mile before he finally fell). So, I guess I can see it.

Somehow the COs didn't even know it happened until they found Moose during night count bleeding out and unconscious in his cell. Weirdest part was he was back on the yard less than two weeks later, and our new rep.

Shorty? After the COs did the camera check, he was placed on a bus, for like ... diesel therapy.

Me? I figured we were going back on lockdown right when the incident happened, so I went to my cell to read and try to get my mind off Billy's situation. I knew it was far from over. COs seldom keep their word.

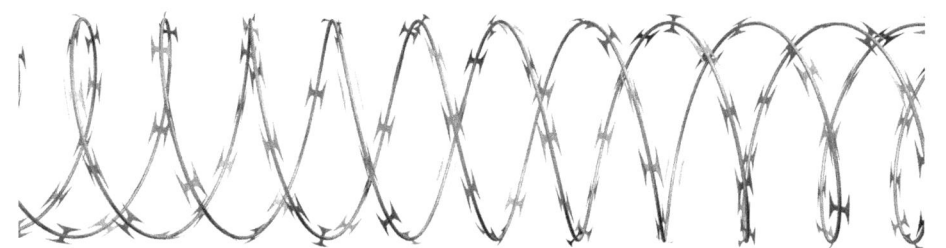

CHAPTER 22

GLEN'S BEATEN SILLY

The bodies were really starting to reek—not even Glen could overlook it. Failing to realize, in his delusional state, the extreme difficulties of getting them back up the stairs, the bodies one by one continued to tumble.

"Next, Marge Dixon, 1247 E. Sandcastle Way. The nosey neighbor." Glen pondered with her driver's license in hand. "Ya know Marge, maybe you should have minded your own business?"

Marge, with her freakish neck vertebrae pointing toward the roof, was actually an easy one. Glen simply parked the wheelbarrow next to her and gave a little shove. She slowly rolled to the side, right into place. At this point, Glen was feeling like a real pro, as he hummed a melody all the way to the basement.

Pushing 10:30 p.m., Glen decided to get rid of the last vehicle, Jason's truck.

"I'll finish this mess when I get back. Jason, I have to run, you need anything?"

Glen waited.

"You have got to be the quietest roommate in the world. I really never knew this side of you. Or wait, maybe you're still upset about the truck? Yeah, that must be it. Sorry again." Glen said on his way out the door.

At 11:04 p.m., he rolled into the lot just south of the border. No one was around. He coasted to the shack and stopped; still no one stirred.

Suddenly, his door flew open, and hands were grabbing him. His knees scraped dirt as the assailants physically threw him to the wet ground.

"Wait, wait," he pleaded as a boot caught the side of his head. His face kissed mud, while three Mexicans, the same three he had previously done business with, beat him silly.

"You are stupid Gringo. You stink too, like death, are you dead?"

They robbed him of every penny he had, which luckily was only $356.

Laughing, they drove away in Jason's truck, leaving Glen to lay bleeding face down in the dark parking lot.

He tried to stand up, his toes sank in the mud. "Not my shoes." They even took his shoes, the special tight ones his friend Bob gave him.

He stumbled and staggered the long quarter mile to the border.

"What happened to you?" The border agent asked.

Learning from his past mistakes, Glen quietly answered, "I blacked out in a club and woke up beaten and broke in the back alley."

The agent chuckled. "Be more careful next time you come down. Have a nice day. ... Next."

Glen flagged down a cab. As he approached, he heard a horn toot.

"Oh, here's my ride now."

"Geez, what happened to you?" The familiar cab driver asked with a grin.

"Just take me home, please," Glen said with his shirt held to his still trickling nose.

He got home at 2:36 a.m., plopped down on the couch physically, mentally, and emotionally drained.

"Did *you* have something to do with this, Jason? I told you I was sorry." He hollered from the living room.

The following morning, Glen winced when he raised his hand to his pounding head. Every inch of his body ached. He laid in pain, staring at the ceiling, and thought, *well, at least I got rid of the vehicles. Maybe today I can get some holes dug.* He tried to rise and fell back to the couch, *or maybe tomorrow?*

"Jason, you're going to have to cook for the two of us today."

"What's that?"

"Okay, okay, calm down. Wow, who woke you? You aren't still upset, are you?"

"I know."

"I'm sorry."

"Yes."

"Yes, I do."

"No."

"I can't believe you sometimes."

"I can't lay here and argue with you all day."

Glen painfully drug himself to the shower. The water stung his cuts yet felt good on his aching body. He got dressed in his usual black attire, poured himself and Jason bowls of cereal, and sat down at the table.

"What's that smell? Have you showered lately? I mean, I don't mean to be rude, but something really smells." Glen looked around the floor at the two remaining bodies, not counting Jason of course.

"Maybe I should get rid of these before I go look for labor? No, better yet, it'll give me something to do while the Mexicans dig. What do you think?" Glen waited.

"Yeah, I think you're right. Okay, you watch the house. I should be back within the hour." He slurped his cereal. "You haven't even touched your breakfast. How thoughtless of me. Do you even like Rice Krispies?"

Jason, of course, sat expressionless in front of several days of soured plates and bowls that somehow Glen failed to notice as he continually pushed one aside to be replaced with the next. "You seem really quiet today. Mind if I ask what's wrong?" ...

"Okay, maybe you're not ready to talk about it. I understand." Glen finished his breakfast, pushed his bowl onto the already overcrowded countertop, leaving Jason's where it sat, in hopes maybe he would eat it later, and headed for his car.

Driving through the neighborhood, his old stomping grounds, the place he grew up and once called home, things began to take shape. Not in memory, as one would think. No, this was more like new stuff, things he saw last week or even as recent as yesterday. The work crew on the corner, the library, the elementary school, the shopping center. Glen was starting to feel at home, in a *deja vu* way. He belonged here.

Home Depot was less than ten minutes away. Mexicans were lined up. "Good thing I came early."

Several Hispanic eyes were on him as he pulled into the parking lot. All of which turned away once they confirmed it was indeed him. Glen trolled the line in search of interested candidates and or the familiar face he had previously dealt with.

There he was. The two locked eyes before the little Mexican quickly turned away. At the same time, others, basically everyone followed suit.

Glen came to a complete stop. No one approached his car.

"You work?" He asked through the passenger window. Some stood and stared; others stayed turned. No one came to his car. A truck pulled in behind him.

"Eight –I need *ocho*." The first eight in line nearly climbed over Glen's car to get to the truck.

"Move, *andale, andale!*" a Mexican yelled while clapping his hands overhead.

Glen slowly rolled away.

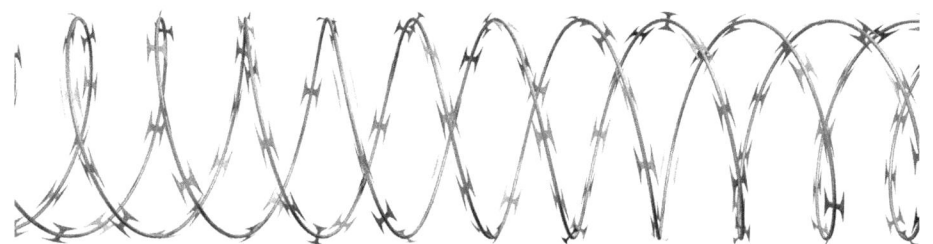

CHAPTER 23

BILLY'S UNFORTUNATE FATE

C how time came like clockwork, as it always does in prison. Still wanting to visually distance myself from the troubled Billy, Glen and I waited until he was off the tier before we came out of our cell. We saw him as he boldly entered the sally port, with his blue prison-issue shirt blowing in the wind. The gunners saw him as well but didn't say a word.

By the time we got off the tier, across the dayroom floor, and through the sally port, Billy was walking in the chow hall.

"Hey, tuck your shirt in."

Billy stood in line, facing forward, completely ignoring the officer.

"You."

The chow hall gun tower guard shined his light on him. "Tuck your shirt in." The CO working the door yelled for the second time.

Metal clanged as the tower gunner snapped his rifle's action into place. People spread out, leaving distance between them and Billy.

"Tuck your fuckin' shirt in, asshole."

Billy, now standing alone, stared into empty space.

"Down!" The CO yelled.

The entire chow hall, except Billy, all hit the ground just as the alarm sounded.

COs ran, jumping over us, ten plus deep, as they all tackled little Billy to the ground. He's lucky trigger–happy Brooks wasn't in that tower. Brooks probably would have dropped him dead. Anyway, off to the Lieutenant's office, he went.

We finished our meals and marched single-file with ten feet separating each one of us, on top of an eight-inch curb, all the way back to the building, as we did every meal, every day.

"Why didn't you tuck your shirt in?" the Lieutenant, the same Lieutenant Billy saw earlier, asked. "I … um, I thought …"

"You thought what? It's a simple question. Why didn't you tuck your fuckin' shirt in? Do you understand simple English?"

"I… thought …"

"You thought nothing!"

"Peters!" the Lieutenant yelled, "Take this inmate back to his unit."

Billy stood confused.

"And the next time one of my officers tells you to do something, you do it! Understood?"

Billy nodded his head.

Back in the building, I was pushing a broom, completing some extra duty I received a few months back when I saw Billy being escorted from the LT's office. By chance, I was sweeping near the sally port when he entered. Splat, I heard the unmistakable sound of flesh hitting concrete. I stopped a couple feet shy of the entrance.

"Where the fuck you think you're at? This isn't Camp Fuckin' Snoopy."

I saw Billy pressed against the wall just as the CO punched him in the side. The air went out of him. "You're going to do what the fuck you're supposed to do, or I'll kill you myself! You hear me motherfucker?"

The CO hit him again in the side. This time he gave him a knife, leaving Billy no choice but to accept it. "Tonight, asshole," the CO said as he yanked Billy off the wall.

I felt I had just witnessed a heinous crime, a CO crime, a CO murder. All I could think about was getting away from the sally port before they came in the room, a mere ten feet away. Drawing the unwanted attention of his co-worker, I quickly slid across the room, with my broom gathering dust and debris as I went.

"Wilson," the gunner said through the gun slot, "Lock it up." It was like everybody, the floor cop, the gunner or gunners ... *everybody* knew what was going on ... everybody but Billy.

I parked my broom and went to my cell.

"Dave," Billy whispered.

"Yeah, I know."

"No, listen, that cop—

"I know Billy, I heard him. What did the Lieutenant say?"

"He played like he had never seen me before."

"The same guy?"

"Yeah. I'm scared, Dave, real scared. I don't know what to do."

Bad thing was, I didn't either. I mean, what do you tell someone who you've already told he should PC up, and they wouldn't let him? I had never seen anything like it. Here you have a youngster saying he's in fear for his life, and you have guards who are paid to protect us, telling him they will kill him unless he takes a life. This was a very bad situation in a very bad place.

"Listen, Billy."

I heard the ripping of material, I assumed to be sheet.

"Billy?"

I got no answer.

"Billy, what are you doing?"

Rip … ripppp …

"Billy, listen to me."

Rip … ripppp …

I looked up at Glen. He had lowered his book to his lap. "Don't do it, Billy!" he said as he rose to a sitting position.

The tearing stopped.

"Billy."

Nothing, he wouldn't say a word.

Two, maybe three minutes passed.

A picture of Billy and his mom, the picture everyone knew, the picture he was so proud of, came sliding from under his door. I heard him say, "I love you, mom, and I'm sorry."

These were the last words Billy would ever say.

Gasping for the air, he couldn't breathe. His feet hit the wall vibrating through to my cell.

"Man down!" I screamed. No one paid any attention.

"Man down! man down! Hurry! man down!" I yelled at the top of my lungs while his twitching spasmodic body continued to beat the walls.

Finally, a CO stepped out of the office.

"Hurry, hurry!" I yelled.

He chuckled and said something to the other cop who still sat at his desk.

Both gunners stood and stared while the two floor cops laughed.

I continued screaming. "Do something! You rotten pieces of shit, do something! Man down!"

The wall stopped vibrating as the rotten stench of urine, feces and death consumed the area.

I slid to the ground in frustration and cried. There was absolutely nothing I could do. So, I sat and wept like a small child.

Glen went back to reading his book. Being his thirteenth year, he had probably seen similar things before. He was the cannibal. I had to remind myself. Eventually one of the COs moseyed his fat ass up the stairs.

"Yeah, he's dangling. I think he's gone. Let's get a medic up here." He said as he casually walked away, eating a sandwich.

Billy hung for the next hour and a half before help finally arrived and cut him down.

"Ya know, you probably could have said something." One of the medics said to me as they were rolling Billy's body away.

"Fuck you!" was my only reply.

Completely oblivious to what actually goes on in supermax, the medic walked away, shaking his head. Everyone, COs, medics, everyone stepped on the picture until eventually, it was close enough for me to grab.

Billy had written on the back, 'I love you, mom.' This made me tear up some more. I think it may have got to Glen as well. Emotionally exhausted, I laid on my rack and slept right through chow.

I woke at midnight and began to read.

By the way, the following morning, an all too familiar face paid tributes next door and took Billy's pedophile of a celly away. Let's just call it, the Inland Empire car paying their respects and demonstrating they were indeed a force to be reckoned with.

In my opinion, that was the only good thing that came out of this very ugly situation.

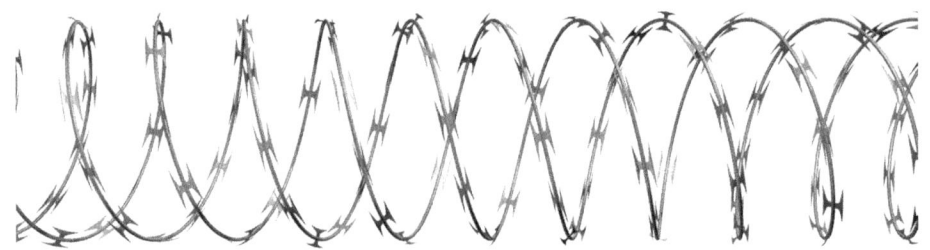

CHAPTER 24

JASON, THE CHAINSAW, AND THE AX

Not quite sure what the problem was, Glen tilted his rearview mirror to get a look at himself. Two black eyes, several cuts, and contusions, basically normal in Glen's eyes. Normal for the past few weeks anyway. Confused, he drove home to seek other avenues.

"Maybe burying bodies in the backyard wasn't such a good idea after all? I'll ask Jason what he thinks!"

"He hasn't done anything with that hole."

"Evelyn, please." Her husband barked as he sat watching *The Andy Griffith Show*.

"I'm just saying," Evelyn whined from under her binoculars. "Don't you think it's a little weird?"

"What's a little weird?"

"That he dug a hole, well, or has a Mexican dig a hole, then he doesn't do anything with it?"

"No, I don't."

"Oh, here he comes now," Evelyn said like a kid glued to a mystery movie or a nosey neighbor watching with binoculars.

"George, George, here he comes."

"I don't care."

"He's got a shovel. Now he's just staring. Don't you think that's weird?"

"Um, no."

"He's going back inside."

"Evelyn, stop it!"

"He just looked straight at me," Evelyn said as she hid around the corner.

"You'll be lucky if he doesn't call the police on you. Now stop it!"

She peeked through the drape.

Glen stood and pointed at her when she turned around.

"Oh my God! George, George, he's pointing straight at me!"

Scared, she ran to seek comfort from her grumpy irritated husband.

"Jason, you need to go talk to your neighbors before they end up on top of Marge."

Glen sailed the last two bodies downstairs, grabbed a soda out of the fridge, and plopped down on the living-room couch. He reached for the TV guide and screamed. "You scared me; *how* did you get in here?"

Jason sat smiling his faceless grin on the couch right next to him.

"Don't scare me like that. I nearly had a heart attack. Seriously, *when* did you get in here?" Glen flipped through the guide.

"Okay, what do you like to watch? We have *Gilligan's Island* at 7:00, I kind of like that show. There's *Leave it to Beaver* at 3:00. What do you think?"

He got up to change the channel.

"*Leave it to Beaver*? Are you serious? Wow, we just keep learning more about each other every day."

Glen knew the bodies had to go. Where and how was the problem.

"First, I'll dissect them. Much like the frog in science class. I can do that." He got up and walked to the basement door. The stench nearly knocked him off his feet as he stumbled backward into the wall and kicked the door shut.

"My mask, where's my mask, Jason?" He hollered, "Have ya seen my mask?" Eventually, he found it in the trunk of his car. Now, better equipped with the battery pack hanging off his belt and his mask firmly snugged in place, he went in for the kill.

Bodies on top of bodies, climbing halfway up the stairwell. Limbs, arms, legs, feet, and hands, all poking up at all angles. Heads dangled, some upside down, others upright, almost as if waiting for something.

Glen got a shovel and pushed. This only seemed to add to the problem, causing yet a larger obstruction. Suddenly his foot slipped on the moist step, and he tumbled headfirst into the bodies, then head over heels into the abyss. Retching with his mask down around his neck, Glen sat on the cold basement floor and hacked up curdled milk with partially digested Rice Krispies.

Completely disgusted, he threw his mask to the side and started pulling bodies off the stairs. Once everyone was semi-laid on the concrete floor, he found some plastic under his Dad's workbench and spread it across most of the remaining area. Winging it, step by step, with no real plan in place, he carefully climbed up the now clear, very slippery stairs.

"Yeah, I know. You're no bed of roses yourself, buddy boy." He said to Jason after plopping back down on the couch. "And, if you went through what I just did, you wouldn't smell too good either."

After catching his breath, he went outside to his Dad's small metal shed to inventory his tools. A large ax leaned against the wall. "This should do." A mid-size chainsaw sat on a shelf, next to a can of gas and some rope. "Perfect." He threw the rope over his shoulder, grabbed the chainsaw, ax, and gas can, and awkwardly carried them inside, pausing only to glance toward the neighbor's window, who, of course, was watching his every move.

"You're not going to believe this, George."

"Probably not, Evelyn."

"No, seriously, he just took a chainsaw and an ax inside, for Christ's sake."

"Evelyn."

"What would anybody need a chainsaw and an ax indoors for?"

"Maybe he's doing some renovating?" Did you ever think of that?"

"No, he's not!" she raised her voice.

"Something's going on, I'm telling you."

"Evelyn, please."

"Jason, what do you *think* I'm gonna do with it? Sometimes you ask the *stupidest* questions."

"What?"

"I didn't call you stupid. I'm just saying— think outside the box sometimes is all." Glen sat the items down at the end of the couch and took a seat.

"Look, I'm probably going to need some help, so?"

"Stop yelling at me. Geez, forget I asked."

"Oh, that's a good idea, thank you."

He went to the kitchen to find his dad's electric meat carver. He held it up to the light. "For the little things." Glen chuckled.

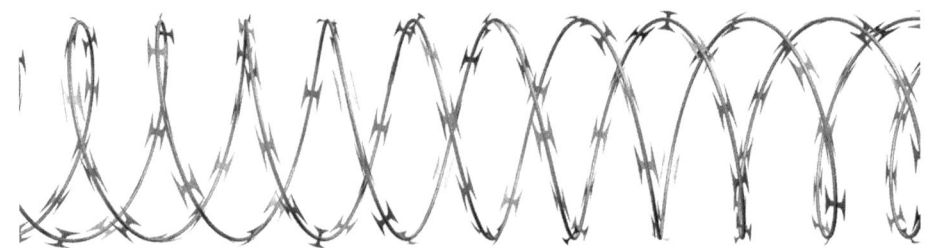

CHAPTER 25

DIVERSITY; A MEANS OF SURVIVAL

Occasionally prison has a way of questioning one's life. Who you are, where you have been, where'd you come from? This was one of those times. Generally, prison life didn't get to me, but Billy's death was cracking even *my* hard shell, probably because I was so helpless.

I had a wife waiting for me. She had been loyally standing by for all these years. At times, I would have to tell myself, over and over, "this isn't real, this isn't real. Out there, the free world is all that matters. My wife, my life, that's what's real, not this."

I saw so many people who lost this reality, who got caught up in the here and now, turning their little term into a life sentence. I didn't want to be one of those people.

Every time I looked at the picture of Billy's mom, it reminded me of my mother, the angel. She tried so hard to divert me from a life of crime. At times relocating, just to get me out of a bad neighborhood.

Even my four siblings followed her suit. All of them hell-bent on leading their baby brother in the right direction. Yet, there I sat. In one of, if not the worst prison in the nation, daily struggling to keep my date and/or stay alive.

My wife, how does she do it? How does she handle calling all her own shots, sleeping alone, eating alone, living alone? How does she pass her day? Sure, she has family, two grown kids, four younger sisters, mom, and dad, but she was still alone.

Being a choice, this lifestyle left little to no room for sniveling. The only question would have to be, why in the hell would anyone choose it? That's a question I, to this day, still don't have an answer to.

People tend to think convicts are all one way, referring to us as "them." They couldn't be more wrong. It takes all kinds to make up the prison population. Just look at Glen, up there reading his book. He and I couldn't be more different. Yet, here we were, in the same cell, living together, playing backgammon together, co-existing with mutual respect for each other.

It was that way everywhere you looked. On one side of me lived Pat Parks, a lifer, and the principal's son, on the other side of him, a bank robber who's done nothing but rob banks his whole life. It worked like this all the way down the tier, across the state, then nation, and probably the entire penal system throughout the world.

In prison, diversity was something we dealt with regularly. To master its' many complexities was a means for survival.

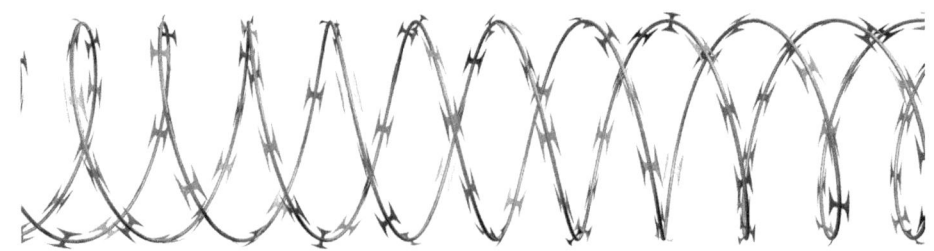

CHAPTER 26

THE NEIGHBOR

Suited up, Glen carefully scaled the depths. Sitting by the workbench was a large twelve-inch thick, fourteen-inch piece of wood. Once he securely positioned the piece on the center of the plastic, he drug Gloria's body across the floor and placed her neck over the block.

The ax felt good in his hands. He swings it back and forth to get a feel of his new tool. "On the third count. Come on, Gloria, count with me." He placed the blade flush to her neck, raised it twice, "Three!" The ax came down and lopped off her head smooth as silk.

Next, he placed her arm awkwardly across the block. He missed his mark, grazed the side of the block, and nearly cut his own foot off as the ax struck concrete, cutting into the tip of his shoe.

"Wooo, wooo, easy now. Slow down and take it easy." Glen told himself.

His second attempt was successful. After some shifting of her body, he carefully sliced off her other arm, both at the shoulder.

Awkwardly holding up one of Gloria's multi-jointed limbs, he decided to further break it down at the elbow and wrist. Somehow three smaller, easier–to–handle parts sounded better to Glen's delusional mind.

He placed the parts, including the head, in a neat little pile and positioned her upper thigh across the block. The leg smothered the block, making guide points limited.

The ax swung. Splat! He swung a second time. Bone crunched. The third missed, grazing flesh and concrete.

Hampered by his gear, particularly the mask, he yanked it off and choked as his eyes and cuts stung.

"Not something I couldn't get used to." He told himself. Glen picked up the ax and swung a fourth time. Now dulled, the axed thudded into the carcass, making little to no progress that he could see.

He swung again and again. Four times in all, splashing his face and body with some kind of horrible funk he couldn't quite identify, before the leg, still attached, fell to the side. Gasping for the fresh air that was far from present, Glen dropped the ax and stumbled toward the stairs.

He paused at the door and looked back. Bodies piled four feet high consumed most of the space. Gloria's half mutilated carcass laid awkwardly across the plastic. Her head or what was left of it lay nearby on top of a pile of arm pieces.

"No, this isn't going to work. I'm going to have to hang some things, – that's it, I'll hang everything up!"

"Jason, order us a pizza, please," Glen said on his way to the storage shed in search of baling wire.

"Honey, honey, here he comes."

"Evelyn."

"Oh, my God, he's covered in something. I think it's blood."

"Evelyn, when are you going to stop this?"

George moseyed over and glanced out the window just as Glen entered the shed. "Evelyn, you're losing your mind. Do we need to make another appointment with Dr. Foster?"

"I'm not crazy! There he is now. Come see, come see."

"I've seen enough, Evelyn."

"I'm going over there."

"Mind your own business."

"Gloria is my neighbor, so she is my business."

"Suit yourself."

"How could you not be concerned?"

"It's not that I'm not concerned or that I don't care, which I really don't. It's simply I don't think anything is going on. So, could you please get away from that window and let me watch TV in peace. Look, Evelyn, *Three's Company* is coming on. Come on, you love that show."

"I'm going over there," Evelyn said under her breath as she continued to look out the window. Consumed by television and retirement, George paid no attention as his wife slipped out the door with her car keys in hand.

Glen kept his car parked down the block and was sure to collect the mail and daily paper off the front porch for this exact reason.

Evelyn drove around the block three times before finally coming to a complete stop in front of the house, Tom and Gloria's house, Glen's house of horrors.

She sat for several minutes, looking for anything out of place, anything suspicious. With her heart beating one hundred miles a minute and choking on the butterflies that swarmed her stomach, she reached for the car's door handle. Suddenly, the tall stranger, now dressed in black from head to toe, emerged out the front door, wiping his face.

Evelyn slowly rolled away and waited down the block, monitoring the stranger's every move. "Who are you, and what are you doing there?" She said in her inner voice.

The stranger, with his long legs, easily covered the short distance to the sidewalk and started walking straight her way. Too scared to move, Evelyn sunk down in her seat and watched the man approach. Glen glanced at the crazy lady, who obviously was trying to hide from him.

Pausing at her passenger window, he raised his hand to knock, then decided against it, as he walked to his car, which unfortunately sat right in front of hers, and drove away.

Evelyn exhaled and grabbed her chest. She wanted to follow this man, this crazy murderous man, this maniac of a man. As her breathing and heart calmed to an octane level, she decided to do just that, at a short, safe distance.

She followed him four cars back, all the way down Rosecrans Blvd, to the Home Depot five miles away. "Did he see me? Did he notice me?" she asked herself, over and over again.

Glen parked near the front door and went in to buy the baling wire he couldn't find in his Dad's work shed.

Evelyn parked in the outer parking lot and waited, for what? She wasn't sure.

Seventeen minutes later, Glen emerged carrying an orange Home Depot bag. He scanned the parking lot on the way to his car and wasn't surprised to find the blue Ford Taurus with a silver-haired lady just sitting there behind the wheel. Glen got in his car and opened the glove box in search of writing material. After locating an old True Value pen and paper to match, he drove toward the Ford.

"Oh my God, oh my God. He's coming this way." Evelyn sunk as low as she could with the top of her grey head still poking up. To her relief, the man paused briefly at the back of her car and sped away.

Nearly too shook up to drive, Evelyn eased her car out of the parking lot and raced for the secure comfort of her home.

"George, George, you're not going to believe this."

"What now?" George, who paid no attention to her even being gone, asked.

"Listen to me, George. He's a murderer, a killer, a maniac. He's like seven feet tall, and he has two black eyes with cuts and scrapes all over his head and face."

"So, What! Maybe he's some kind of fighter? Did you ever think of that?"

"No, he's too old."

"Maybe he's been in an accident, like a car wreck or something, and he's there healing? Stop it, Evelyn!"

"He threatened me!"

"And how did he threaten you?"

"He stopped at my car window. I thought he was going to break it."

"Break it?"

"Well, maybe he was only going to knock on it. But I'm telling you, he's dangerous, and he scares me."

"Okay then, stay away from him."

Evelyn grabbed her binoculars and headed to her window to continue her surveillance.

After getting gas and a pizza, Glen drove around the block in search of a license plate on one blue Taurus that read California 271BMT. "Just as I suspected, another nosey neighbor," Glen told himself as he finished trolling the block. "That's okay. What's a couple more basement visitors?"

Once again, he parked down the block and walked home.

Glen sat the pizza down on the coffee table in front of Jason and said, "Oh good, the pizza's here. How much was it?"

He reached for his wallet, "I'll reimburse you. No, I got it. How nice of you. What? Well, okay, if you insist. Hold on, I'll get us a couple plates." He went to the kitchen.

"Look,—baling wire." He pointed to the orange sack.

"I'm gonna hang parts. What?" Glen waited.

"I know it's genius. How's your pizza?"

After Glen consumed two and a half pieces, he looked at Jason's untouched plate and said, "Ya know, you really don't eat much. Are you okay?" He chuckled as he got up, wiped his mouth, and changed into some work clothes.

Holding one end, he tossed the roll of baling wire over one of the 2x4 beams that supported the roof. He repeated this maneuver ten more times, leaving twenty-two dangling wires. Next, he picked up Gloria's head and plopped it down on the workbench. The eyes were basically gone. To clear a passage, he inserted his finger through the eye socket until he felt a clear path to the other side.

Once this was complete, he swung the head, holding it with his middle finger through the socket, and giggled, rocking it back and forth. After he finished playing with his new toy, he bent a twelve-inch piece of wire, like a fishhook, and snaked it through the eye holes. He then twisted two small eyelets at the wires' ends and carried the head across the room to be hung face-up six feet off the ground.

"You see something interesting up there, Gloria?" Glen snickered.

Now he picked up one hand and two arm pieces and walked up the slippery stairs to the garbage disposal. Swollen with decomposers, nothing, hand, or limb would fit down the sink's hole. He stepped back downstairs to get the electric meat carver.

Back at the sink, the meat carver didn't cut bone, like, at all. Glen grabbed a hacksaw and eventually cut off the fingers. One by one, he carefully fed them into the hungry appliance. The disposal grumbled and grunted as it struggled with the tiny finger bones.

Jamming twice, he forced the blades using a hammer handle. Glen smelled burning wires as smoke emitted from the drain. Finally, it spun smooth. He turned it off and carried the remaining parts back downstairs. While there, he grabbed the second hand and went back to the disposal.

With blood, gore, and bone fragments spread across the kitchen counter, the garbage disposal gave one last screaming protest before freezing to a complete stop. Glen tried the hammer handle with no luck as more smoke flowed from the hole. The poor machine was burnt.

"Shit! This being the first curse word Glen had muttered in many years. He turned off the machine and went back downstairs.

He physically tried to pull Gloria's leg from her torso. Stubborn threads made this near impossible. He chopped more with the dull ax, still nothing.

Eventually, holding the leg up the best he could, he cut the remaining tissue with the meat carver. The carcass rolled to the ground. Exhausted, he stumbled over the block and fell in a sitting position in the muck, right next to what was left of his precious mother-in-law. Glen sat on the cold, wet plastic next to the stack of stinking decayed bodies and pondered his situation.

"This isn't working. I need to get organized."

He decided right there and then, he needed to dismember all the bodies and sort the parts in an organized fashion. "I'll hang all the heads, and I guess the legs too. Jason's going to have to give me a hand. That's all there is to it!"

His soaked pants stuck to his body, as he pulled himself off the ground and climbed the stairs, headed for the chainsaw.

"Ya know Jason, this wouldn't be near as hard if I had some help … hint, hint," Glen said as he picked up the chainsaw. Gas trickled onto the couch, carpet, and coffee table when he poured a small amount of the pungent fluid into the little reservoir.

"What a mess."

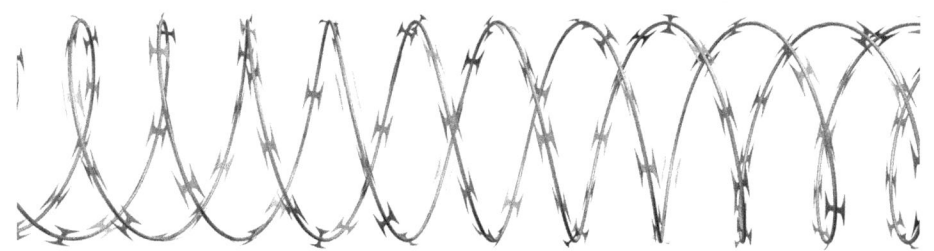

CHAPTER 27

THE LIFERS' MOUSE

The following morning, still disturbed by the nasty unfortunate chain of events that ended Billy's short-lived life, I reluctantly drug myself to work. The shop, sweatshop if you will, was a large metal warehouse containing a variety of 400 plus sewing machines, elasticators, and button pressers. Just about every machine ever made to create clothing was in that building.

These machines were set up in six long, two machine rows, each governed by a lead-man. I myself ran a five-spool Juki overlock sewing machine, running a thousand miles a second, all day long. A hundred feet of polished concrete separated us sewers from the cutting tables.

Only lifers worked the tables, which was pretty ironic, being each and every one of them possessed a series of fourteen-inch razor-sharp tools, ranging from scissors to punches. I don't know if it was an attempt to keep us in line or simply how it was. But I gotta say, there's something intimidating about a dozen convicted murderers standing in front of you with a fourteen-inch pair of shears.

Anyway, these lifers captured a small rodent, a mouse to be exact. They made him this little cage. Now, what I'm about to tell you is going to go against every prison movie you've ever seen, but like I mentioned before, this wasn't a very nice place.

These lifers tortured that poor little mouse every day for nearly two full weeks. At the end of each day, after shooting staples into his head and body and removing something, an eye, another ear, whatever, they would hang him with a paper clip through his shoulder blades, suspending him in mid-air inside his little cage.

The following morning, they would hoot and howl as they squared up their bets placed on the poor little guy's endurance or lack thereof.

My machine sat at the end of the line, directly in front of the cutting tables. Witnessing this gross state of ignorance was unavoidable as I watched the mouse's refusal to succumb to his adversaries. Finally, somewhere around the mid-point of the second week, I could take no more.

Disrupting my entire line, I shut my machine down, stood up, brushed myself off, and with every eye on me, I walked over to the cutting tables.

At this point, I was completely out of bounds. Not only did lifers run the cutting tables, they were the only ones allowed over there. Everyone, meaning the whole room, stopped and stared.

"With all due respect, guys, really?"

Two lifers, one nearly seven feet tall, the other five feet nothing, came forward with scissors in hand and asked, "What?!"

"The mouse, come on, man, what did he ever do to you?"

The short guy's face twitched and contorted as he glared through gloss black eyes, as dark as the swamp he no doubt crawled out of, "What did you say, mother fucker?" he barked.

Now here's the thing. Most lifers run with nobody other than lifers. Basically, they surrender their flag at the gate. Where they're from doesn't much matter being they're never going back there.

So, here I have this guy. He looks white. I have no idea where he's from, who he knows, or what he's done, other than he's a lifer, simply because he's on the cutting table and he's really pissed off, holding a fourteen-inch pair of sharp cutting shears by his side.

"I'm just saying, enough already, put the little fucker out of his misery." I pleaded.

The dark-eyed maniac came forward while raising his scissors. Now less than a foot from my face, he looked up and growled through clenched teeth, "check this out mother-fucker" small drops of spittle slung from his mouth, "I got six life sentences. And, if I want to torture some fuckin' rodent or any other motherfuckin' thing, then that's what the fuck I'm gonna do! Nobody sweats mine!" He raised his scissors and voice, "Do you understand me?"

Okay, scared I was not, but in the wrong, I was. I mean, the man had a point. It's a rodent, not a person or even a dog or cat. What the hell was wrong with me?

Time froze. He glared, I stared. Not quite sure how to get out of this, I slowly backed away and returned to my machine. For several minutes the lifer stood and stared until the tall one said something that brought him out of his angry trance, and the two went back to work.

It seemed every time I looked up, he stopped and glared, oozing hate and anger my way.

That night I told Glen the story. He said, "That's Tim Broach. He came in with three life sentences, caught three more for killing people inside. I can't believe you're still alive."

I don't know, maybe I had a death wish or was just plain stupid, but that night I made a plan. The following morning, hell-bent on carrying out my mission, I marched to work like the brainless soldier I had become. Sitting at my machine, I waited patiently for all the cutters to arrive. Tim Broach being the last to clock in.

With my heart racing through my ears, I got up, left my machine on, being I didn't figure I would ever see it again, and walked straight to the mouse's cage before they got him out for his morning ritual. Everyone, cutters, sewers, packers, everyone froze. Wasting no time, without as much as a pause, I opened the wire door, reached in the cage, unclipped the little guy, and bit his head off. Just like that, I bit it right off.

It was warm and crunchy. Not bitter like one would think. I never looked at the lifers behind me, who all stood in stunned disbelief and stared. I just tossed the body to the floor and walked away, chewing the little mouse's head.

Staples stabbed my gums, causing me to wince secretly as I continued to chew all the way back to my machine. Never as much as looking up, I grabbed a piece of orange fabric and started to sew.

I heard my neighbor sitting next to me chuckle, "Fuckin' Dave," as his machine too began producing jumpsuits a thousand miles a minute. Followed by others, within seconds, the entire shop was back in motion.

Eventually, I glanced toward the tables. Ironically Tim Broach, the killer, the psycho, picked up the rodent's lifeless body, turned to face me, smiled like a demon from hell, and popped the remnant of the poor little fella right in his jaws. As he chewed, he opened his mouth several times to show me specifically the furry gore as it slithered down his throat.

Bottom line. Looks like I would indeed live to see another day.

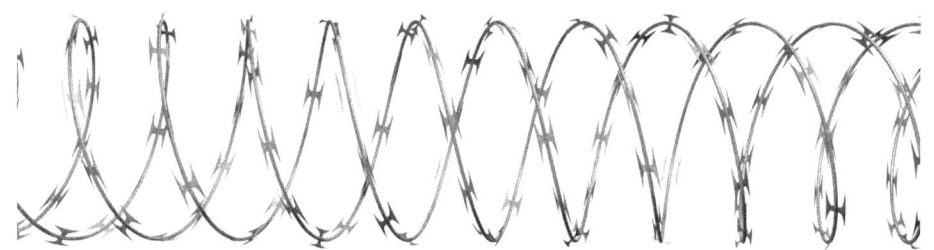

CHAPTER 28

BAGGING UP THE BODY PIECES

F ailing to change, off to Home Depot he went. He cruised the block and paused briefly in front of the nosey lady's house. "She definitely has to go. The only question is, how?" He quickly raced away.

"Contaminate their water. I sure like that idea. I'll see what Jay-Jay, that's funny, I wonder if he likes that? Anyway, I'll see what he thinks when I get home."

Glen parked and walked towards the front entrance. Suddenly a lady screamed as people started running away. Confused, he waltzed inside the store. Two kids screamed; people were running into each other, trying to get out of his way.

"What the—?"

Glen finally glanced down and realized he had forgotten to clean himself up before leaving the house. His entire front side was covered in blood, bone, cartilage, and rotten human funk. Self-conscious, he raised his hands in a futile attempt to cover himself, as if he were naked, then froze in place while everyone stared. Glen turned and ran out of the store.

Screeching out of the parking lot, he noticed at least two good samaritans trying to catch his license plate number. He raced home. "Jason," he hollered through the foyer, "Why didn't you tell me I forgot to clean up. I must look horrible."

Glen jumped when he walked into the bathroom and saw himself in the mirror. Thirty minutes and a shower later, now suited in his black attire, he laughed… "Can you imagine what those poor people must have thought? Like I'm some kind of monster, for Christ sakes."

Deciding on a different Home Depot, Glen thought, *The El Cajon store will do*. He traveled the fifteen-minute drive in peace, listening to his favorite tranquility cassette. This one being the sounds of the sea, "Eeeh," the whales sang.

Inside the store, his black eyes drew unwanted attention but at least no one screamed and ran. After choosing an electric chainsaw, the best the store had to offer, and a shiny new ax, he searched for someone to assist him.

"Excuse me, sir, do you know anything about these?" Glen held up the saw.

"Yeah, what do you need to know?" the young employee asked.

"Well, how strong are they, you know like, what can they handle?"

"What are you cutting?"

Not quite prepared for such a question, Glen awkwardly shuffled his feet, placed the saw back in his basket, and said, "nothing, I mean just some yard trees, branches, you know."

"If you're cutting oak or any other hardwood, I would suggest a gas-powered unit, something by Husqvarna perhaps."

"Yes, well, see, I was concerned about ventilation."

"Ventilation in your yard?"

"No, yes, well, I have asthma, you see."

"I see. Well then, the electric unit should suffice."

"Thank you, sir." Glen limped away, leaning on his cart.

The man stood and stared until Glen was out of sight.

"What's up?" a passing by co-worker asked.

"You ever get the feeling like something just wasn't right?"

"All the time."

"Yeah, me too, but this time was really weird. I mean, the guy just looked all crazy, and he's buying a chainsaw and an ax?"

"So?"

"I know. It was just weird, is all."

"Maybe you should report it?"

"Report what? That somebody just bought an ax and chainsaw?"

"Exactly. Have you taken your break?"

"Not yet, whatcha got?" The two went about their day.

$936.53 later, he had one box of super-duty trash bags, some extra plastic, a couple pair of goggles, just in case, a super heavy-duty rubber bonnet with matching gloves that covered his entire front side from head to toe, a new shiny ax, an electric chainsaw, and, he nearly forgot, one new garbage disposal.

"Jay, I'm home." Glen chuckled. "I think it's funny when I call you that!"

"What?"

"Why?"

"Okay, okay, I'll stop"

"No, I don't want you to call me Gee."

"I said I'll stop."

Glen ate some stale pizza while making fun of Jason for losing weight.

"I'm just pointing it out as a friend. You're getting a little thin. Now you'll have to excuse me, I have work to do, and you're obviously not going to help."

Minutes later, decked in his new gear, Glen stepped into the living room and asked through his full facemask, "So, what do you think, Jase?"

He quickly raised his mask, "I can call you Jase, right? I mean, you don't mind, do you?"

"Okay, thank you, so, what do you think?"

He plopped the mask back over his face. There he stood all six and a half feet of him, bald head, face hidden behind some WWII chemical mask with a single canister screwed to it and a shiny black rubber bonnet hung by shoulder straps that draped to the ground. "Well, what do you think?" he asked for the second time as he raised the chainsaw.

"I know, ha."

He picked up the new ax and headed down the stairs. Hampered by his bulky gear, he carefully, step by step, explored the depths, when suddenly down he went … Bam, bam crash, splat, he found himself breathless, laid out across the plastic-covered floor.

"Ouch!" He held his knee like a boy who just crashed his Schwinn. After a brief moment, he pulled himself off the ground, picked up the chainsaw, gave it a once over, flipping it this way and that. Surprisingly, it looked okay. He grabbed an orange extension cord hanging on the wall, plugged it in, and hit the switch.

The machine sang to life. Glen liked the feel of it, the power, the force. Each time he hit the trigger; the saw jumped in his hands.

Eager to play with his new toy, he pulled the remains of Gloria's carcass over and easily lopped off her remaining leg. On a roll, he made a cut at the knee and one at the ankle. The saw breezed through flesh and bone like a warm knife cutting through butter.

"This is simple," he told himself as he kicked Gloria's carcass out of the way and grabbed the next body in line. Fluid sprayed, flies swarmed, and sparks flew as the blade made contact with the floor, time and time again. The pieces quickly stacked up.

Blinded by the gallons of rotting human fluids that poured from every surface around, he pulled a rag from the workbench and unsuccessfully attempted to wipe his mask. He sat the saw down, took off the mask and gloves, and looked around. The entire basement floor was covered in parts. Rotting, decayed, swollen human parts.

"Jason, you gotta see this." He yelled up the stairs.

He cut the baling wire and hung the heads next to Gloria's with roughly twelve inches separating each one, all of which stared at the rafters. With that project complete, he picked up his bottled water off the workbench, splashed a small amount on his facemask, wiped it clean, put the mask and gloves back on, and continued his work.

An hour later, with hands, arms, and leg pieces piled on one side of the visqueen, and the swollen torsos laid side by side on the other, Glen took a break to assess his situation.

Grim, he thought as he looked around. The torsos were cumbersome to move. "I'm gonna have to break these down too." Using the electric shears, he cut twenty fingers off two sets of hands. Looked around the room, found no simple way to carry them, so he started stuffing them in his pockets, with intentions to feed them down the garbage disposal—you know the one he had absentmindedly forgotten to install?

He hung his bonnet on a nail next to the mask and very carefully, still dripping with slippery fluids, attempted to scale the stairs. The fifth step got him again, this time hitting his chin on the way down.

"Shit!   (Sorry.) You didn't hear that Jason," he hollered from the basement floor.

"Darn it," Glen whined when he saw the unit unopened, sitting amongst the rotting food on the dinner table. Fingers trickled out of his pockets as he awkwardly tossed and turned under the sink. Burdened by his mental and physical state, the simple installation was harder than it probably needed to be.

Glen took a small mallet and smashed the finger on the kitchen counter, hoping to break the little bones. Smack, splat, crunch. Pieces flew all the way across the room.

"A pillowcase. I need a pillowcase." He shoved the remaining sixteen or so fingers in a pillowcase; he got out of the linen closet and went to town with the mallet.

"Now this, this works pretty good." Having cracked and broken several countertop pieces, which Glen had no concern whatsoever, and with the water running and the machine in full cycle, he began pouring the pillowcase contents down the drain. Clump, clump, two large clumps, the second being the largest, wobbled down the hole. The unit, just like the old one, grumbled and growled in protest of its over-loaded boney content.

Screeching to a smoldering halt, Glen quickly shoved the mallets handle down the drain. The unit spun, yanking the hammer out of Glen's slippery hands. Immediately breaking the blades, the motor came to a smoking stop.

Foaming gore boiled to the top of the drain— "Damn it!" Glen barked. He left everything, mallet, pillowcase, gore, where it sat and plopped down with all his exhausted weight right next to Jason on the couch.

"Whew,— this is some work."

"My chin?"

"I took a little fall, is all. But thank you for asking."

Glen picked up a piece of fly-covered pizza with his blood-stained hand and started eating it.

He grabbed the trash bags and some knives, including the one he killed Ricky with, and headed back downstairs. This time he actually descended sideways, one step at a time, and still nearly fell, as he caught his balance and cheered when he reached the bottom unharmed. He flipped the first torso face up, "that's funny face up," and with a sharp shearing knife, he made a cut from the neck down to the navel.

This exposed the white cartilage breastplate. Glen rapped three times on the plate with his knuckles. He turned and set down the knife and picked up the chainsaw. Clogged with drying matter the chain was reluctant to spin.

Glen tapped it twice to the ground, freeing the blade. The saw sang true. Like some kind of deranged doctor, he carefully cut the decomposing cartilage with ease. Shocked, Glen stared as withering maggots fell to the floor.

He placed the additional six carcasses in similar positions and went down the line with the knife, followed by the chainsaw. Once this was complete, he rolled them over, one by one, and basically poured their contents, with little resistance, to the floor. Glen was standing in a swamp, as the wet organs, with miles of intestines, quickly flowed free, covering the entire floor.

He picked up each of the gutted, armless, legless, headless bodies with ease and snaked baling wire through their hip bones, before hanging them from the rafters. Aside from the disgusting black swamp river and the stack of limb parts it somehow flowed around, Glen was pretty happy with his work thus far. Certain he would slip and fall, he hung his mask and bonnet and crawled out of the basement.

In the shed, he found a short-handle large-scoop shovel and a Rubbermaid plastic trashcan and headed back inside. Somehow Evelyn wasn't at her window, and she missed seeing Glen at one of his goriest yet. From the top of the stairs, he threw the trash can and shovel to the depths and spider–crawled back down himself.

Next, he lined the trashcan with a bag and started the gross tedious task of shoveling human muck. Within minutes the bag was full, so full he couldn't lift it out of the can. Using the shovel, he scooped some out. Five bags later, and down to mere inches of muck left on the floor, Glen was thoroughly exhausted.

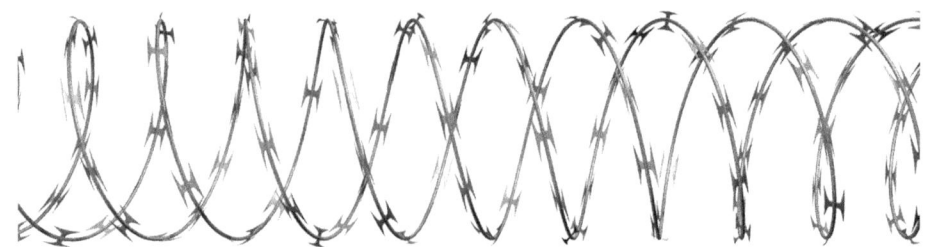

CHAPTER 29

THE IE CAR TAKES OUT SPANKY

After several days in the infirmary, which apparently the Warden felt to be enough punishment, Moose was back on the yard. "Fuck dude," I said, "You look like someone stabbed you or something."

Moose was covered in tape and bandages. His yellowed skin hung loose on his bones. "That little fucker almost killed me."

"Yeah, I guess we won't be seeing him anymore."

"I know—I heard they put him on a bus."

"They did."

"That really sucks. I tried to say I fell down the stairs and hit every sharp corner on the way down, but of course, they didn't buy it."

Obviously enjoying his newfound authority, Moose got serious and said, "Listen, Dave, they're moving some dude from Idaho or Nevada or some shit in Billy's old cell today. Tom, Tim, Gary—I don't know, anyway, shortly thereafter I'm moving one of our homeboys out of the gym in there. He's a youngster named Taz. I think you know him?"

"I do."

"Anyway, give the kid a heads up, would ya?"

"Of course," I answered.

It's strange how inmates know everything going on in prison, from who's coming, who's going, what they're carrying, and what they're about.

Sure as the sun rose, Tim or Tom, possibly Gary from someplace, who knows where, moved in next door, and of course, Taz was soon to follow. Today was Saturday. After a good workout, I went to my cell to relax.

"Dave," Taz said through the vent.

"Yeah, Taz, what's up?"

"Tim, my celly, just called Spanky from IE, a *punk ass bitch* over some card game.

"I didn't hear any shots?" I said.

"No, that's the thing. Spanky didn't do shit. He just stood there and stared."

"No shit."

"Yeah, I think they might be coming in here to deal with it. I mean, I saw his homeboys sweating him. Oh, here they come now."

I looked through my door. Tim (apparently), my neighbor, just came through the sally port with Spanky, a short distance behind.

"Taz," I whispered through the vent, "When the cop comes back around right now, go take a shower or something."

Tim stood facing his locked door and stared at nothing while he waited for it to open. Spanky stood about twenty feet away, looking really nervous. The CO opened the door. Taz quickly stepped out as Tim stepped in behind him. As the door began to close, being automatically controlled by the tower, once the CO turned the key, Spanky quickly slipped through the narrowing crevice.

"You ready?" Tim asked.

"Listen, bro, I didn't want to fight you, but my homeboys are sweating me. So how 'bout we just hit each other a couple times to make it look good, and you know, call it a draw?"

"What? Man—fuck you, dude."

Crack!!! I heard Tim hit him.

"No, no, wait, wait, I give, I give. Come on, bro, I had enough."

"What? Man— get up, sissy."

"No, I've had enough."

"What the fuck?"

"Please?"

"Check this out, you fuckin' fag, you lay there in the corner like the coward you are until the next unlock, then go tell your homeboys what a fuckin' twat you are. You hear me?" Tim jumped at him with his fist balled up.

"Yeah, yeah, I'm sorry, come on, don't kick my ass, dude."

"Fuck you."

Not a sound came from that cell for the next hour.

That night Spanky's stupid ass told the IE car exactly what happened, *but* with the roles reversed.

"You should have seen the pussy cowering in the corner like a little bitch. I probably could have fucked him if I wanted." Everyone laughed.

All he had to do was be quiet. Tim wasn't going to say anything, and Lord knows I wasn't either. But no, he had to go run his mouth.

Tim? I kinda liked the guy.

"Neighbor," I asked through the vent.

"Yeah"

"San Diego, name's Dave. Where you from, dawg?"

123

Washington, Washington State, name's Johnny. I don't know why these stupid fucks keep calling me Tim."

"That's funny."

"Yeah. Did you hear that little fucker?" He asked.

"I did. Thank God he's not from Dago."

"Or Washington," Johnny chuckled.

Anyway, the next day, of course, the IEs were trying to tax my neighbor Johnny.

"Are those clowns serious?" Johnny asked.

"Yeah, well, I don't think they're getting the real story. If they were, Spanky would no longer be with us."

That afternoon Johnny went to the yard and got pulled over by Tiny, the IE rep.

"Dude, the fellas want a thousand dollars placed on someone's books today. Is that going to be a problem?"

"Check this out, Tiny, was it?" Johnny didn't wait for a reply. "I don't know what that fuckin' lame is telling you, but I assure you, you're being misled. I ain't the one."

"Do what?"

"Yeah, fuck that punk, next time you shoot him or any other lame up in my house, they're gonna scrape them up on a gurney. You hear what I'm saying?"

"Easy, dude."

"No, I'm serious. I wasn't going to say shit, but that little sissy is leaving me no choice." Two laps later, Tiny said, "Listen, dawg, let me look into this, and we'll get back to ya."

"Yeah, meanwhile, don't send nobody in my house," Johnny warned.

"No, no, don't trip, homie. Hey, are you going in right now?"

"Probably soon Why?"

"Well, when you do, could you shoot Dave out? I need to have a word with him."

"No problem, see ya, Tiny."

"Yeah, that's what I suspected," I told Johnny after he ran it down to me.

"And Tiny said he wants to talk to you."

"I figured that too."

Ya, see, here's the thing. I'm not one for telling. However, if I don't tell Tiny what happened, then IE is going to move on Johnny, my new friend. Spanky brought this on his self, and even though Johnny's not from San Diego, hell for that matter, he's not even from California, I have to tell the truth.

As I came out of my cell, Johnny was standing at his door. The look on his face said it all. The look of a misplaced soul, far, far from home. The look of being all alone, thinking Dave couldn't go against someone from Southern Cal, for one that wasn't even from this state.

"I got you, bro," I said as I passed by his cell.

Johnny didn't say a word.

"Tiny, What's up, homie?"

"I'm good, you?"

We walked a couple laps while I explained what I heard and even saw and witnessed straight through the vent. Tiny shook his head and exhaled at least twice during our little walk. Eventually, he lowered it in shame.

In supermax and even lower levels, everyone wants to be from the best hood. Best, basically being the toughest, most stand-up fellas on the yard. A weak link means a break in your chain. It makes everyone in your whole car look bad like they don't take care of theirs, like they're all weak, spineless wimps.

"Tiny, I hate to be the one saying this. I really wish it had happened somewhere else, or not at all."

"No, I know Dave. We'll deal with ours, and I'm sorry for the trouble."

"No problem, Tiny."

"Hell, I guess I owe that dude. What's his name?"

"It's Johnny. He's from Washington State, and I like the cat."

"Yeah, I kinda do too. Anyway, looks like I owe him an apology?"

"He smokes Bugler." I smiled

Tiny chuckled, "Cool, I'll see what we can do."

Everyone from IE knew what was going on, well, everyone except Spanky, that is, as he waltzed out of the silkscreen shop where he worked and entered the little hallway that every day inevitably led him back to the yard. Four of his homeboys came through the door, another three came from behind.

"Spanky, what's up, dawg?"

"Not much. Tiny, what's going on?" Spanky's voice cracked.

"I think you know."

His homeboys jumped him while Tiny pushed open the door to the woodshop, which, unfortunately for Spanky, was unlocked. Once inside, with Tiny's giant hand covering Spanky's mouth, the IE car began the very painful bloody task of removing the 'White Pride' off the back of Spanky's arms, followed by the stubborn 'Inland Empire' that was chiseled across his chest in solid bold black letters. Spanky tried to scream as he squirmed, wiggled, and moaned in agony while they peeled layer after layer of meat from his tortured body.

Eventually, prior to their final scrapes, he lost consciousness. His homeboys left him lay.

The following morning the woodshop instructor nearly tripped over Spanky's body before he realized he was standing in half-dried blood.

No one knows the actual time of his death, nor does it really matter, I guess. Fact was, another mother had a broken heart, and IE had completely redeemed themselves.

Lockdown and time to read.

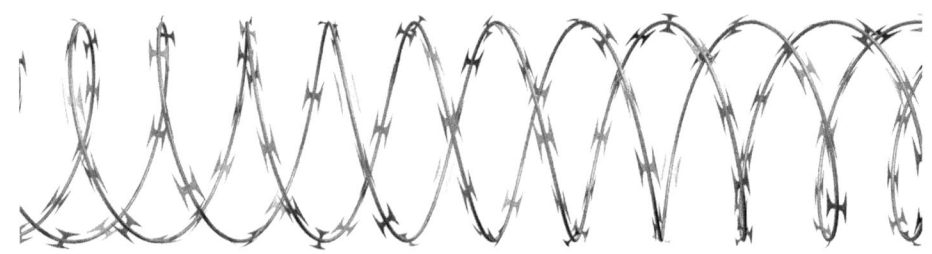

CHAPTER 30

BOATING

After slipping on the steps, not once, but twice, and somehow hitting his face not twice, but three times, Glen felt half beat to death when he finally emerged from his dungeon and carried himself straight to bed, fully dressed, muck and all. At this point, the disturbing stench of rotting death could be detected all the way to the sidewalk. Ten long hours passed before Glen woke up and painfully pulled himself out of bed.

"A shower. Do I need a shower?"

"Jason, do you think I should shower? What? Shut up. You're always making jokes."

Glen carried himself to the kitchen. "Boy, what a mess."

The fluid level had gone down some, leaving several orange crusty stain lines behind. He looked down at the sink. Stagnant blood and debris remained.

To change the motor, once again he had to get the fluids out. For lack of a better idea, he went to find a hose. After scouring the grounds and coming up empty-handed, he cut a few feet off a black commercial-grade garden hose he located in the shed.

"George, George— hurry. Oh my God, George, come quick. He looks like, like something really bad, hurry!"

George, in an attempt to appease his wife, finally came to the window. "Let me see." He said very unenthusiastically with his hand outstretched for the binoculars.

"Wow, I guess that does look pretty bad," he said as he adjusted the sights.

"I told you. Now can we call the police?"

"The police? No. Just because someone doesn't look right in their own back yard certainly doesn't call for the police."

"But look at him."

"I am, and no, we're not calling the police.

Back inside, Glen placed one end of the short black hose in the sink and draped the other over the counter towards the floor. Unfamiliar with the whole siphon process, he wiggled the hose and waited with a large stew pot as if something was going to come out. He wiggled it again. Nothing.

As a boy, he one time saw his father siphon some gas out of an old tractor. It was so long ago, and the fuel seemed to flow so easily.

"What did he do? Hey Jason, have you ever done this before?" He hollered over his shoulder.

"Seems as I remember, Dad had to suck on the end of the hose to get it going? Yeah, that's what he did."

Glen raised the hose to his lips and reluctantly gave it a pull. Nothing. He tried a second time, still nothing. He checked the opposite hose end. It had cartilage, bone, and blood clots stuck to it. He shook them off, replaced the end back in the muck, and gave it one big final suck.

Suddenly, pieces of horribly rotten bone and cartilage shot down his spasming throat while fluids gagged him as they burst out of his nose. Glen pulled the hose aside and vomited while nearly choking to death. Temporarily free of its obstruction, fluids sprayed all over Glen, the floor, the wall, down the cupboards, and somehow even on the counter overhead.

Coughing, choking, and fighting for air, he grabbed the hose and shoved the end in the waiting pot. One chunk, it slowed, two chunks, it slowed even more before coming to a trickling stop. Gore was everywhere, but in the pain, tears ran down his face, his mouth, tongue, throat, and sinuses burned like he had swallowed battery acid, which in essence, he had.

Using the counter for balance, hacking spit, and stomach bile, he staggered to his feet and peered down the sink. "How ... how could it look the same?" He glanced at his surroundings, then back down at the sink—lower, but not quite empty.

Frustrated, he decided to pull the garbage disposal anyway. After wiggling into position and loosening the retainer screws, fluids began to drip down his arms. He grabbed the stew pot, quickly removed the screws, and pulled the unit free.

At least a gallon of gore smacked him in the face as clotted blood, bone and cartilage spewed, saturating the cupboard and kitchen floor. Retching, Glen crawled away with the motor in hand. He dropped the unit on the living room floor and fell next to Jason on the couch.

Jason's head slowly rolled to the side. "Oh, fix your head. That looks ridiculous." Glen reached for the pizza that was now several days old. The box was empty.

"I see you finally ate something. That's good, I was starting to worry."

He looked at Jason, whose head was now upright.

"Thank you, that's way better. You hungry? I'm having cereal. What? I know, Captain Crunch for you."

Glen returned minutes later with two bowls; both had chunks of curdled milk on top. He ate both bowls, turned toward Jason, and said, "I'm so glad you're finally eating again. Maybe soon you can help me with my chores?" He paused.

"I know, I know, just relax for now. I've got work to do."

"What the—?"

Three torsos had come free and were awkwardly lying about. Even more disturbing were the plastic trash bags, swollen up like giant balloons, plump and ready to pop. Like his life, Glen's little house of horrors was beginning to get out of hand. Even he, in his extremely delusional state, could see this.

Back in the living room, he mulled the state of the basement.

"Jason, I really need your input here." Glen looked long and hard at his friend.

"What? Okay, see, now that's a really good idea. Thank you. I'll start right away."

The plan was Dad's boat.

"What better way than to feed the sharks?"

In the yard's far corner, Thomas stored his twenty-seven-foot Cabin Cruiser. Glen went to make sure it was still in operating condition.

Everything looked good, just as Glen remembered it. His Dad's truck, a 1979, three-quarter ton Chevrolet, sat next to the shed. Aside from a dead battery and expired tags, it looked to be in operational order. Ironically, after some extensive searching, he found the keys to both in Jason's top dresser drawer.

"Why didn't you tell me you had the keys? You probably could have saved me time and hardship."

After hooking up a battery charger, Glen started looking for equipment. He grabbed a large ice chest out of the shed and found everything else, life jackets, fishing tackle, buoys, all in the boat.

Walking in the house, with the ice chest in hand, Glen glanced toward the nosey neighbors.

"You see, you see what I mean. He's doing something. I'm not sure what, but he's doing something, George."

"Yeah, he is a weird one," George said, peering through the binoculars.

"And, what's all over him? What is that? It's even on his face."

"I'm not sure. But like I've said, maybe he's doing some remodeling, like maybe a bathroom?"

"No," Evelyn gawked through her less powerful lenses, "You know that's not true!"

George lowered the glasses and walked back to his lazy boy.

Evelyn continued to stare.

Having stepped down in the basement, Glen sat the ice chest on the concrete floor and slid over one of the torsos. After slipping back into the rubber bonnet, finding the mask to be unnecessary he picked up the chainsaw and easily quartered a carcass. This worked well, so he quartered them all.

Minutes later, with this task complete, he sat some parts strategically in the chest, using limb pieces to fill in the gaps. With the container half full, he cautiously carried it up the steps and placed it by the front door. He held up his hands, looked himself over, and said, "Maybe I should shower?"

The water level rose as clots challenged the drains capacity. Eager to rid himself of this mild distraction, Glen pushed them through with his foot. Now clean and decked from head to toe in his Johnny Cash disguise, Glen headed for the truck.

It started instantly. With it comfortably idling, he got out and removed the boat's block and cover. He eased the truck out of its slip and carefully backed up to the boat. The trailer hitch lined right up, "smooth," he said to himself as he slowly pulled the boat out of the garage.

"George, he's doing something."

"What now?" George asked on his way to the window.

"Something with the boat."

"So, what!"

"Look, look at him."

"I am, and now you're just being nosey."

With mere inches to spare, he vigilantly eased the truck, boat, and trailer down the side of the house. Once out front, he left it running, got out, dropped the tailgate, and loaded the chest in the back. He slammed the gate and paused to assess his surroundings.

Content no one was watching him, no one he could see anyway, he did a quick last-minute inspection on his rig before he, his dad's two-tone blue '79 Silverado, and the twenty-seven-foot Chris Craft Cabin Cruiser slowly rolled away.

"I like this. It was a really good idea. Thank you, Jason." Glen yelled over his shoulder as he headed for a gas station.

"I'm envious," the man pumping gas next to him said.

"Pardon me?" Glen nervously asked.

"The boat. I would give my left nut to be going fishing right now."

Glen replied, "Really?"

"Well, maybe not my nut, probably a hand though, like maybe my left hand." He held up his hand and smiled.

Glen suddenly realized the man was joking, "Oh," he chuckled, "Yeah."

"What is this, a twenty-nine, thirty-footer?" He walked toward the truck and trailer.

"Yeah, hey, um, could you back a little?" Glen's voice cracked.

"Wow, take it easy, guy. I mean no harm."

Glen stood his ground. "Just back up."

The man backed off, hopped in his car, and shook his head as he drove away.

After paying for gas for both truck and boat, he bought a large bag of ice in an attempt to cover the parts. This looked pretty good. Pulling out of the gas station, he heard a horn, followed by screeching tires.

Scared and confused, he looked up just as a police cruiser came to a sliding stop. The cop hit the lights and chirped his siren, "pull your vessel to the curb." He shouted through his speaker.

Glen's blood pressure exploded through the top of his head. His whole body broke out in a sweat. His hands trembled. "Run" was his only thought as he sat frozen in time and place.

"Pull your rig out of the street and park at the curb, now!" the officer barked for the second time.

"What to do. What to do?" He nearly cried.

The officer hit his siren again. "Sir—please—."

Glen eased forward. He could still hear the officer's loudspeaker but could no longer make it out. He slowly gained a little momentum, dragging the cumbersome boat and trailer through the driveway and across the street where he parked, still slightly blocking traffic.

The officer quickly pulled over and parked behind him, jumped out, and aggressively rushed the truck. Glen was scared, real scared. He nervously sat, too scared to move, still frozen in place.

"Driver's license and registration." The angry officer demanded.

Glen shook.

"Have you been drinking today, sir?" He raised his voice like maybe Glen was hard of hearing. This helped pull Glen out of his trance. He finally looked at the officer.

"Drinking? I don't drink."

"Step out of the truck, please."

Glen paused.

"Step out of the vehicle." The officer barked.

Glen slowly opened his door.

"NOW!!"

Sensing the officer was on the brink of violence, Glen quickly complied.

"What happened to your face?" The now curious officer asked on the way to the shoulder of the road.

"My face?"

"Yeah, the cuts, the black eyes, what happened?"

"Car wreck. I mean, I got mugged in Mexico."

"So, which is it?"

"What do you mean?"

"Sir, are you sure you haven't been drinking?"

"No, I don't drink."

"Breathe this way, please."

This was a common early detection system of the '80s.

"Pardon me"

"Your breath … let me smell your breath."

Glen puckered up and blew in the officer's face. The cop stepped back waving, his hands before him. "Jesus Christ, what have you been eating? Do you feel okay?"

Glen looked puzzled. "Yes, today I feel fine," as his nervous stomach grumbled. Truth was, after his little kitchen sink episode, he didn't feel too good, but he wasn't about to tell the police that.

"Sir, have you ever been arrested?"

"Arrested? Of course not."

"Are you on parole or probation?"

"What?—No."

The officer held up the truck's registration. "Who is Thomas Sombers?"

"That's my father. Well, it was my father. He was murdered a couple months ago."

"Murdered?"

"Yes, she killed him. I know she did."

"Sir, are you okay?"

"Yes, fine. Can I go now?"

"No."

"What do you want?" Glen asked.

"Well, for starters, I'm gonna need you to walk this straight line for me."

"I told you, I don't drink."

"Then it shouldn't be a problem now, should it?"

After a series of tests, the officer determined, although strange and confused, Glen was indeed sober.

"So, I can go?"

"No. You can't go. I'm impounding the truck for expired registration. The boat and trailer, however, are currently registered. Therefore, if you wish, I will allow you to pull the boat out of the street and drop it right here, where it can sit for up to twenty-four hours. Do you understand?"

"I do."

"I'm also writing you a ticket for expired tags."

Glen stood and stared.

"You can pull the truck forward now."

An awkward moment passed. Glen found a long-lost shred of sanity. "Officer, I just lost the most precious person in my life, along with my job, my home, and everything I held dear. I've been poisoned nearly to death, beaten, robbed, and fell down a stairwell more times than I can count. All

135

in the past couple weeks, and I promise you, if you could please, just please, look deep down in your heart and find just a little compassion for me, I will get this truck registered tomorrow morning, please."

The officer paused and skeptically looked Glen deep in the eyes.

"I don't do this very often. He paused again. "I trust that you *will* get the vehicle registered as soon as possible and that you *won't* drive it meanwhile. I am, however, still writing you a ticket for registration."

"So, consider it your lucky day. You look like you could use one. Please pull the boat out of the road while I complete your citation."

"I can go?"

"Yes, after I write your ticket." The officer walked away, shaking his head.

After easing forward, Glen impatiently waited, watching his rearview mirror the whole time.

Moments later, the officer returned, "Please sign right here." Glen quickly complied. "Keep it parked. The next officer may not be so nice," he said as he was walking away. God only knows how the officer didn't smell the horrible stench of death that Glen emitted with every breath he breathed.

Seriously concerned about losing his dad's truck, Glen showed absolutely no recognition of how close he just came to getting arrested for multiple homicides, as he patted the seat and said, "almost lost ya old boy," while driving away.

Determined to complete his mission, Glen chose an easy access landing on Mission Bay by Dana Point. He and his father had docked there for years. "Let's see if I can remember how Dad did this?"

He slowly backed the trailer to the waters' edge and jumped out. The truck continued in reverse. Glen quickly jumped back in the driver's seat, put the truck in park, and solidly pressed the emergency brake. With safety now being high priority, he slowed down, grabbed the steering wheel, and said, "Relax and think."

Lately, this was easier said than done, as his life and everything around him just seemed to crumble to dust. He exhaled, got out, and started working the electric winch. The boat slowly crept towards the water. Now floating on its own accord, he walked the trailer rail and released the winch.

The boat started to float away. Glen quickly climbed on board. "I'll have to leave the truck there." He told himself as he glanced towards the Silverado and saw the ice chest still sitting in its bed.

"Damn it!" He snapped. He started the boat, fortunately with no problem, drove in a large circle, and carefully shot onto the trailer. By this time, spectators, a father and son waiting to dock, had gathered.

Both were laughing as Glen splashed off the boat in waist-high water, grabbed the winch clip, and started trying to hook the boat. After submerging twice, the man yelled, "You need some help there?"

"No … I got it." Glen gurgled as his head bobbed up and down. As comical as it was, the man and his son tried not to laugh. Glen finally got the boat hooked and drug himself out of the ocean.

'Now the ice chest?' he pondered with confusion.

"You sure you don't need a hand?"

He couldn't raise the chest high enough over his head to get it on the boat, not without potentially spilling it. "Well, yeah, maybe I could use a little help."

"Wow, this thing's kinda heavy– whatcha got in there, the ex-wife?" The man chuckled.

Startled, Glen stopped and said, "No, why? … I mean, "of course not."

"Hey, I was only joking, my friend."

"Well, yeah."

They set the chest in the boat.

"Anyway, do you think maybe you could go around my truck, like maybe dock over there?" Glen pointed to a nearby landing.

"Sure, I guess. Are you leaving your truck there?"

"Yes, I'll only be gone a short while."

"You sure you don't want me to move it for you. I could leave the keys wherever?

"No, no, right there's fine."

"Okay, suit yourself. You have a nice day."

"Yes, you too," Glen said as he detached the winch, climbed on board, and slowly trolled away.

"That man was kinda weird, dad."

"Yes, he was."

Back at the truck, the off-duty policeman, also known as Detective Carson, picked up his radio. "Cathy, could you run this plate for me." He asked the dispatcher.

After finding neither truck nor boat to be stolen or involved in any reported crime, the officer and his son docked their boat and went about their day.

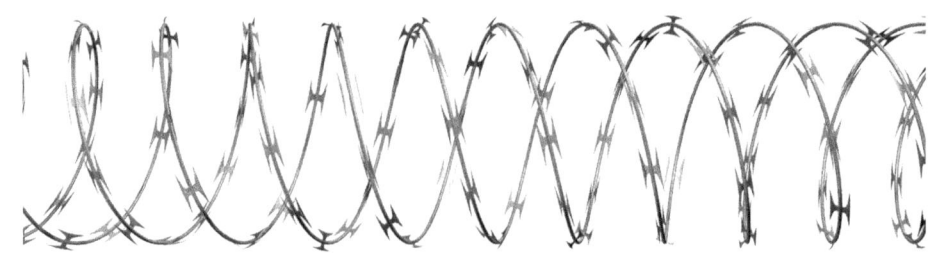

CHAPTER 31

DAVE DEFIES THE SYSTEM

One thing about COs, including the Captain and even the Warden, they are very inconsistent, over-paid, and seldom do what they say. Don't get me wrong, the lockdowns did seem to be getting longer, but were the COs ready to run the prison for a whole year? Let's just say: Not yet.

This one was ten days and about a half-million games of Backgammon, during which time I started asking Glen some questions.

"Why do you figure you didn't get deathly sick after the siphon incident?"

"Truthfully, I was in such a state, I now have a hard time remembering it."

"Would you rather not remember?"

"Well, of course. But it happened. So, I force myself to deal with it, daily."

"Do you mind talking about it?"

"For some reason ... I don't quite understand ... I'm okay with it."

"Okay, maybe you didn't die because possibly you had built up a tolerance to it, and, or, perhaps the poison had a shelf life, so it wasn't as potent as when you first made it?"

"Yeah, maybe."

"Wilson." The CO standing at my door bellowed, "The Captain wants to see you—ten minutes." He unlocked my door and walked away.

"Man, I hate this shit," I whined to Glen as he won the game.

"Why you? Isn't Moose running things now?"

"Yes, he is, and I'm not quite sure."

"Mr. Wilson," the Captain said as soon as I entered his office, "Have a seat." This time indicating a folding metal chair.

"I'm going to get right to the point. Why are you guys still killing people? Do you not believe I'll lock the yard down for a year?"

"No sir, with all due respect, that last incident had nothing to do with San Diego. Also, sir, I'm no longer calling shots and ..."

"I don't give a shit where the hell these white guys are from or who the hell they think they run with. I gave you an order, an order to carry out a message. Did you or did you not carry out that order?"

"Yes, sir, I did, but ..."

"But nothing. Are you talking back to me?"

"No, sir."

"Then, what the hell's the problem?"

"I'm not sure, sir."

"*You're* not sure. Then, *who is*? You certainly don't expect me to talk to this Moose character, do you? ... Well, ... do you?"

"No, I guess not sir."

"Listen to me very close, Wilson. I see here you have about ten months or so left?"

"Yes, sir."

"If this shit doesn't stop, then, not only are you not leaving on your date, but when and if you ever do leave, it will be from the hole. Matter of fact, give me one reason I shouldn't take you there right now, pending investigation for murder."

"With all due respect, Sir, I myself don't do drugs, and I don't gamble. You're barking up the wrong tree. Furthermore, I don't take well to idle threats, so if you're going to take me to the hole, then so be it." I stood up and stretched my hands out in a handcuff position and stared.

The Captain paused.

"Always pushing the line. Aren't you, Mr. Wilson?"

"No, I'm not."

"Sit down."

I took my seat.

"You see, sir, I'm not bucking. I simply don't care."

"You don't care?"

"No, sir, I really don't. I actually don't give a shit if I go home tomorrow or never, ... or if it's from my cell or the hole. I... don't... give... a... fuck!"

At this point, the Captain was smirking.

"I'm not sure why. Maybe it's a result of me being here just too damn long. I don't know, but I truly don't care."

"Mr. Wilson, I'm going to overlook your entire charade here. Mark it off as temporary insanity for say."

"Thank you, sir."

"Tomorrow, we have a bus coming in." The Captain shuffled through some papers. "Looks like... twenty-four whites. Please guide them in the right direction."

"No problem."

I stood up, "Will that be all, sir?"

141

Time froze as we both stood and stared.

"Cooper." He yelled. "Please take Mr. Wilson," he paused again, "Back to his unit," he said to the guard. Even a Captain at a supermax prison, who has to assert his power 24/7, respects a man who stands up for himself.

Thing was, I did care. I actually wanted out, probably more than any man alive. But I had a belief, still have it today, which is, the only true power "the man" has, is the power of the key, the threat to take one's freedom, to lock him or her up.

Contrary to popular belief, this doesn't stop when you go to prison. There are prisons inside prison. Then once you get there, they can mess with your food, your shower, whether or not you have a book to read. But when you take the power of the key away, they have nothing.

So, bluffing? I guess I was somewhat. However, I truly no longer cared about much of anything. That part was no bluff. Truth be known, with everything being so chaotic all the time, the hole kind of sounded like a pleasant change.

The next week smoked right by, and before we knew it, we were back on the yard.

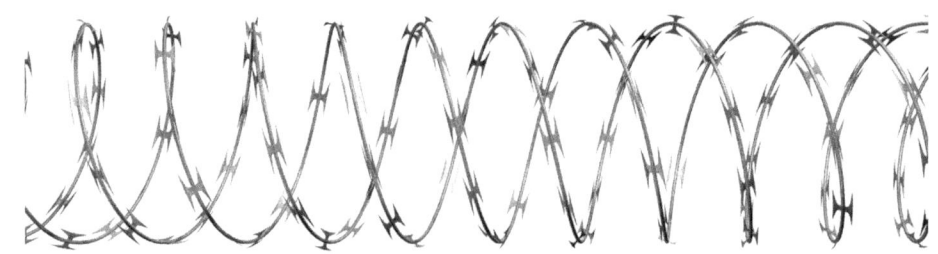

CHAPTER 32

THE STORM

Baffled as to why people yelled and pumped their fists in anger while he made wakes in a no-wake basin area, Glen pushed the throttle, causing the big engine to rumble as he headed for the open deep blue waters of the Pacific. Standing, he braced himself in the wheelhouse as the boat rocked back and forth, often misting his face with refreshing salt water. At one point, a half dozen dolphins swam, keeping pace with his boat.

For the first time in weeks, Glen felt like a real man, a human being. Sanity tried to assert itself, "What have I done?" He asked himself.

A picture of his father and him in this very boat, fishing in Baja, flashed before his eyes. Anger instantly overrode any and all emotions as he pushed the lever to full throttle. The land got smaller and smaller. Eventually disappearing from sight.

With nothing as far as the eye could see, he slowed to a trawling pace. The sea was becoming choppy, tossing the now tiny vessel to and fro. He shut the engine off and, holding the rail for support, carefully made his way to the deck. Up, down and side to side, the waves forced the little boat.

"I just need to get out of here."

Glen picked up the chest. Suddenly the boat keeled to the side, throwing him as it did. The ice chest flew from his grips, spun through the air, and hit the deck on its side, spilling ice and parts everywhere. Glen was slammed with a great deal of force, straight into the wheelhouse.

In the muck, down on all fours, gasping for air, the boat violently pitched to the opposite side, sending him flying through the air, straight into the Pacific Ocean.

In a panic, he stupidly splashed, as his head bobbed up and down, his body quickly filling with the saltwater that was trying to consume him. Tooth and nail, he fought the bitter waters while the boat drifted further and further away.

"Stop it." He tried to calm himself as he went down for what felt like the last time. His hand hit something solid and instantly grabbed it. Unable to sink, the ice chest bobbed like a cork, up and down, while Glen clung to its side and started aggressively paddling towards the boat.

For the next thirty minutes, he swam for his life with one hand while he hung to his life-preserving chest with the other. Finally reaching the bobbing, blood-streaked bow, he couldn't grab the rail to pull himself out of the frigid water. Hanging on to his precious, yet pathetic life, Glen desperately paddled for twenty more agonizing minutes, stroke by stroke, guided by the sheer instinct to survive.

He finally made it to the stern. Spent, he could barely pull himself up. Clinging to the rail, he crawled out of the water and fell face-first to the deck where he choked, purging saltwater out of his nose and mouth.

The second time he was nearly sucked back out to sea, Glen realized, regardless of his physical condition, his recovery time was over. He pulled himself to an upright position and looked around. Human parts bobbed up and down, often disappearing from sight, then hauntingly returning seconds later.

"I have to get out of here." He told himself over and over as he crawled, sliding from side to side to the ladder that led to the wheelhouse. Shivering from head to toe, Glen was jerked all around, hitting his head several times.

The waters were worsening by the second. Click, his seatbelt snapped into place. He cranked the engine and hit the throttle. Guided by his compass, being barely able to see, he headed for land.

Eager to rid himself of this nightmare, he once again raced through the no-wake basin. People yelled. He didn't know why, nor did he care.

Eventually clearing the last piling, Glen saw the San Diego Harbor Police were at his truck. He trolled the area waiting for them to leave, wondering what they wanted in the first place.

Once they'd gone and the coast was clear, he quickly docked and secured his load in place. Sopping wet and happy to be back on dry land, he turned his heater on high, removed a ticket from the windshield, hit his wipers, and finally headed home, pulling the boat and trailer, just as the rain began to fall.

Too distressed to recognize the smell and feel of fresh rain, being something San Diego didn't get near enough of, Glen haphazardly parked out front and stumbled into the house.

Wet to the center of his bones, he drug himself to his already soiled bed and fell face-first into a deep solemn sleep.

Bam, bam, bam. Glen's head pounded. Bam, bam, the sound faded to a knock. He cracked an eye. 11:43 a.m., his bedside clock read. The knock came again. Someone was at his door. He slowly pulled himself out of bed and took a leak before answering it.

Knock, knock, "they certainly are persistent, whoever it is."

He went to the door and looked out the half-moon glass insert and saw no one. While he stared, the knock came again.

"What the?"

"Excuse me, sir, would you like to buy some chocolate?"

Glen looked down. Holding a box of almond chocolate bars in one hand, trying to cover his nose with the other, stood a young boy selling candy for his school.

Glen looked confused as he glanced around.

On the sidewalk stood this kid's friend and obvious partner in this venture, with his shirt pulled halfway over his head.

"Sir, would you ...?"

Stripped of his resolve, the youngster choked as he backed away, too scared to turn his back on this monster.

Both kids ran.

"Did you see his face?"

"I know, and the smell?"

"Yeah, he must have like, a hundred bodies in there." The kids ran for three blocks before they slowed and skeptically began knocking on doors again.

Glen slowly closed the door, turned, and caught himself in a full-length mirror. "I do look bad," he said to himself, with his cuts, scraped, two black eyes and soiled wrinkled clothes, not to mention stubble all over his head and face. "Oh well, I have work to do." He headed for the basement.

"Jason, you think you could handle putting something together for breakfast? You're going to have to start doing something around here, other than sitting on the couch smiling."

His eyes burned, and flies swarmed, actually impairing his vision as they relentlessly attacked his face. Even the sound from a million little wings, all racing to go nowhere, made concentration near impossible as they vibrated the walls, like the steady hum of an airplane in full flight.

With his hands waving the pests away, Glen made his way to his mask, hanging on the wall and gasped when he focused on his surroundings.

Somehow, in spite of his chilling, life-threatening, heroic efforts, everything—the limbs, the torsos, the bulging bags—everything had grown to near double in size.

"How could this be possible?" He asked himself. "Maybe the nosey neighbors have something to do with this? I'm truly going to have to deal with them, sooner or later."

Frustrated, he dragged himself back up the stairs and asked Jason, "So, what are we eating, pizza again?"

Glen picked up the phone he had violently ripped out of the wall weeks before and started dialing.

"Hello, yes, I would like to order a pizza." What do you want on it, Jason? Oh yuk, no way. "I'm just going to get the regular. Okay, thank you, how long, right, thanks again." Glen hung up the broken phone. "It will be here in about thirty minutes."

Forty minutes later, after catching the morning news, noon edition, with Jason, he looked out the window, "Where is this guy? I guess I'll have to go pick it up myself. Jason, you want to ride along? Yeah, that's what I figured. Have you always been such a homebody?"

"Hey neighbor, you're kind of blocking my driveway here." A man who had just rolled his trash to the curb said.

Glen looked up; the man stepped back defensively. Glen paused before fishing the truck keys out of his pocket. "Sorry about that. I'll move it right now."

"Thank you. Hey, you wouldn't know anything about that odor, would you? The man pinched his nose.

"Odor?" Glen asked as he jumped in the truck before the man could reply.

Tap, tap the man gently racked his knuckles on the truck window.

Glen sat and stared.

The guy made a rolling signal with his hand.

Glen reluctantly lowered his window.

"I'm Bob. I live next door," the guy paused.

Glen stared.

"Is Gloria or Jason around?"

Glen still said nothing.

"We haven't seen either one of them for a week or so."

"Vacation" Glen said under his breath.

"Vacation?"

"Yes, I'm house-sitting." Glen rolled the window back up and slowly drove away.

While circling the block, he paid close attention to his nosey backyard neighbor.

One car, the same one that followed him to Home Depot, sat in the driveway. The curtains were drawn; basically, the place looked pretty uneventful.

"This should be a breeze." He told himself as he slowly drove by.

Back at the house, the neighbor "Bob" was just rolling his third and final can, to be placed in a perfect line, right next to his drive. He stopped what he was doing and watched. Glen carefully maneuvered the boat down the side of the house.

"Keep it up, nosey," Glen said to his crazy self.

"George, hurry— here he comes."

George sat down the remote and very unenthusiastically slowly made his way to the window.

"See, see, I told you."

"Told me what? The man is parking a boat."

"Don't you patronize me."

"I'm not. I'm just saying, give the guy a break." George said as he walked away.

Glen stepped out of the truck, turned towards the window, and pointed straight at Evelyn.

She squatted low to the ground, covered by the windowsill. She raised her hand to her heart and winced, "George, he looked at me and pointed straight at me."

"I don't blame him. Every time he looks up, there you are."

"He pointed at me," she gasped.

Glen slid through the house and out the front door, headed for the local pizza joint.

"Is my order ready?" He asked the confused cashier.

"Your name, sir?"

"Sombers."

"Um, no, sir. Did you call it in? I'm sorry, sir. What is it you ordered again?"

Glen placed his order and used the thirty-minute window to purchase his third garbage disposal in a week from a hardware store just a couple blocks away.

Flies swarmed as he opened the front door. Things were becoming unacceptable, even by Glen's standards.

He pushed cups, bowls, and empty food boxes onto the floor and sat the pizza in front of Jason. Wading through the mass of flying parasites, he made his way to the basement door.

"Jason, you left the door open. You're going to have to be more careful in the future." He slammed the door closed and mumbled under his breath, … "or you'll find yourself down there with your family."

What? Stop it, you know I didn't mean it. You sure have good ears, though. Come on, let's eat."

Flies swarmed out every hole in Jason's body, attacking Glen's eyes, nose, mouth, ears, and pizza the second he sat down. He futilely swatted them away as they continued their relentless attack. Once again, reaching his breaking point, he tossed his slice of pizza back in the box and quickly made his way out the front door.

He ran his hand up and down his front, back, and sides trying to rid himself of the lone survivors that desperately clung to his clothes.

Free of this task, he glances up and saw his next-door neighbor, Bob, completely perplexed, staring from his porch. Glen quickly regained his composure and walked to his car.

Twenty minutes later, he bought several boxes of fly strips from the nearby grocery store. In his delusional mind, this was some kind of cure.

Back at the house, once again wading through millions of flies, he sat the garbage disposal on the kitchen floor and began hanging strips. Frustrated and confused with flies still dive-bombing him every time he turned around, he bumped face-first into one of the annoying sticky strips, which ironically grossed him out.

"My mask, I need my mask!" He choked after one or more flies flew down his throat. With his mask now in place, Glen opened the pizza box back up. Flies flew like a Jack-in-the-Box pinging off his glass face-shield.

He looked at Jason, who showed little to no signs of disturbance.

"We need a new place." His muffled voice came through the filter canister, "and I know just the one." Glen peeked out the back-door window and there she was, patiently waiting for his return. He headed for his father's service pistol.

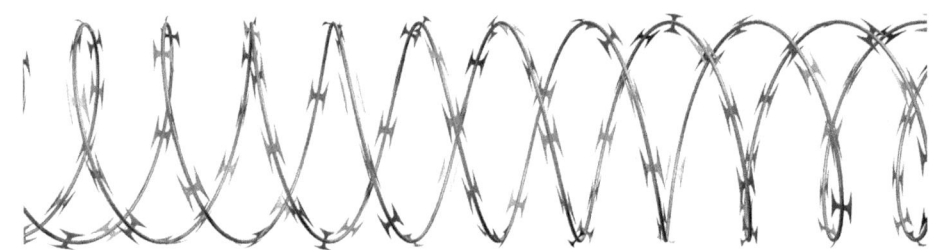

CHAPTER 33

FIVE DAYS IN HELL

That night, right after count, a CO came by my cell. "Wilson, you have outside medical tomorrow. Get ready; you're going to isolation for the night. You can't take anything with you. I'll be back in five minutes to take ya."

"Excuse me, sir, I think there's been some kind of mistake. I have nothing pending."

"Look, I don't know anything about that. Says here you do. So, I have to take you."

Sometimes, usually for surgery at the local hospital, you had to go to the hole the night before, basically to make sure you didn't eat anything past midnight. Thing was, you couldn't take as much as a book, toothbrush, nothing with you.

Anyway, around thirty-five minutes later, the CO returned, and off to the hole I went. With people yelling out the cracks of their solid metal doors and fishing line, made out of torn sheets running everywhere from the top tier to the bottom, and over a hundred feet all the way across the room. The place was an absolute insane madhouse.

The officer took me to an abandoned corner section and shoved me in a cell with a broken toilet. Before I could protest, he was quickly on his way.

Sitting on the metal rack where a thin mattress should have been, was a rolled-up sheet and blanket. The smell was intoxicating. The toilet, clogged and broken, was half full of urine and feces. The floor had pieces of dried toilet paper all over, obviously from the last overflow.

All the water to the sink and toilet was turned off, along with the central air conditioning unit. That meant the temperature was at least 100 degrees. Ironically, I had seen worse. I told myself it would only be for one night and started making my bed on the metal rack.

Before I could even unroll my linen, the light suddenly went out. I had somehow forgotten, lights out at 9:00 p.m. sharp, in the hole. In complete darkness, I threw the blanket down to cushion the hot hard metal and used the sheet as a pillow. Sleep was restless as I tried to roll on my side all night long.

With no clue of the time, I finally heard voices and the clanking of food slot doors dropping. I knew mine would not be one of them, however. This told me it was somewhere around 5:00 a.m. Soon the transport officers should be there to get me.

Several hours passed. No one came.

"Maybe I'm misjudging time?" I said to myself as I peered out the vertical slot window in my door.

My throat was already starting to get sore from the acidic stench that so engulfed me.

More hours passed.

Food slots dropped for the noon meal.

"Maybe it's an afternoon appointment?"

152

I dozed off and woke to the familiar sound of clanging metal. Dinner time had arrived. No COs were coming in my area, being no one but me was there.

I started yelling out of my cell, trying to get someone's attention. Both the officers looked my way, then ignored me while they continued feeding inmates. I beat on my door and hollered. Within minutes the COs were finished and gone.

Discouraged, I sat on the uncomfortable metal rack and waited for count to plea my case. Several more hours passed. I heard the distinct jingling of keys. I hurried to my door and waited for the guards.

After counting the whole room, top and bottom, they paused at the open gate that led to the area I was in. I yelled. They looked, then left.

"Wait, wait, I'm not supposed to be here. There's been a mistake." I yelled over and over as I beat on the door in frustration. I heard the entrance door open, close, and lock. They were gone. I was stuck in the hell hole another night.

Sleep was worse than before. My throat and sinuses were now painfully raw and being dehydrated certainly didn't help.

Morning finally came. The same exact thing took place. The COs fed and left, ignoring my cries for help.

The entire day was identical to the first. Nighttime came. No cops came near my cell. Once again, I was stuck for the night.

Distraught, without a clue what to do and not as much as a book to read, as I stared at the walls, I heard something at my door. At first, I thought it was simply one of the many rodents from the night before who no doubt felt I had totally invaded their space. I laid and stared at the upper graffiti-covered bunk when I heard it again. I glanced toward the floor just as a pop tart attached to a line came flying from under my door.

Startled, I jumped to my feet and snatched the little pastry off the ground. It came with a note. "Dude, why do they have you in that area?"

I had nothing to write with. I tried yelling out my door, but I couldn't get my hoarse voice to travel. It looked like thousands of fish lines spread across the room. Then, the one lone line that stretched out from all the others and went straight to my cell quickly disappeared. "How the hell," I asked myself.

These guys were good, real good. Some of them had been there literally for years, fishing with their make-shift lines night and day, 365 days a year, eventually reaching perfection.

I had no idea where the pop-tart came from. But after a couple days of no food or water, nothing, not one single thing has ever tasted as good as that little pastry. And I don't even like pop-tarts!

I was living Ground Hogs' Day. COs came, fed, and left. At 4:30 p.m., they counted, and sometimes during the day a pop tart came flying under my door.

Day five, thinking I may have to drink my own urine today, I woke to the sharp, high pitch sound of metal to metal. I slowly turned my head towards the door and saw the Captain standing in my window slot. Tink, tink, tink, "Hey, tough guy, do you care yet?"

I got up and walked to the door, "you think this is pretty funny shit, ha?"

"Yeah, I guess there was some kind of mix-up or something."

"Whatever. You done playing games yet?"

"Games? Hum"

"You're not going to break me, Captain. People been trying my whole life."

The Captain chuckled, "we'll see if we can get you out of there." He paused, "maybe today."

"Thank you, Captain," I said on my way back to bed.

Roughly an hour later, I woke to my door opening.

"Pee-yew," the CO waving his hand in front of his face, "damn, how long you been in here?"

"I don't know, a day, a month? Too damn long, that's for sure." I said on my way out of the cell.

"You must have really pissed someone off?"

"Yeah, the Captain," I smirked.

I walked straight to the water fountain; nothing else really seemed to matter.

"Dave," I heard a familiar muffled voice coming from one of the cells.

"Dave, over here."

The officer was in his office, probably doing some last-minute paperwork.

I walked towards the shouting inmate.

"Over here, dawg."

I now recognized Pac-man's distinct voice. "Dude, what the fuck?" I asked.

Pac-man was in a one-man handicapped cell with a little room to maneuver his wheelchair. "Fucked me up, bro. They say I'll never walk again." He twirled his chair with the front wheels off the ground. "I've gotten pretty good in this thing, though."

"What are you doing here? Are you coming back to the yard?" I asked.

"No. I'm waiting to transfer to a medical facility. You?"

"Just the Warden playing his little punk ass games. I think I'm going back today."

"Cool. You get the pop tarts?"

"Oh God, yes. Those little fuckers saved my life. The COs haven't even been feeding me. Thank you, dawg."

"Yeah, we saw that. Hey, don't thank me. Thank my neighbor."

I stepped back and looked next door. None other than Shorty was smiling through his window. "Shorty, what the fuck? I heard you're on the bus?"

"I am. I just got here a week ago. Been all over the place. They told me this morning I'm leaving today."

"We tried to shoot you some coffee, but we couldn't get it over that far. Them fuckin' pastries really fly!" Pac-man said.

"Wouldn't have done any good anyway. I had no running water."

"Wilson," the guard bellowed, "get the fuck away from there before I make you a resident!

"I gotta fly guys. Good seeing the both of you and thanks again."

I glanced toward my little hell hole on my way out, and taped to my door was a fluorescent orange sign that read in big, bold black letters—

"CAUTION QUARANTINE CELL"

Goosebumps ran up my arm. Imagine all the heinous infectious diseases, besides the obvious I had been subjected to, while I wallowed in that 100-degree shit hole of a cell. For five of the most miserable longest days of my life. This being a perfect example of prison inside of prison.

Back at my house, eating a soup and crackers while Glen was at the yard, I was truly happy to be back in the comforts of my cell.

Glen's face lit up when he squinted through the corrugated door.

"You're back."

"I am."

The door opened, and Glen came in.

"Man, I can't tell you how happy I am to be."

"What happened?"

"Long story. I'll run it all down to you later. What's been going on here?"

"Not good, not good at all. A couple of days ago, you know that big black guy who's in the wheelchair?"

"Yeah, Big Jim, I believe they call him."

"I think so. Anyway, he was in the chow line, running his chair, more than once, into one of the skinheads. Actually, I'm not sure if he was a skinhead, but he called this Big Jim guy a worthless nigger. So, the guy waited for him outside the chow hall and when the white guy walked by, the guy pulled himself out of his chair and kicked the white guy in the ass."

"Oh shit."

"Yeah, so the white guy swings on him, and knocks him over backwards, jumps on him like he was going to kick his ass, then he stopped, got up, the two yelled back and forth as the white guy walked away."

Glen crawled up on his rack.

"So, I take it it's not over."

"Apparently not. Rumor has it, Whites and Blacks are rioting tomorrow morning."

"Let me guess. They wanted to hit commissary first, is the only reason they haven't yet?"

"Probably."

"Okay, I'll go see what I can learn."

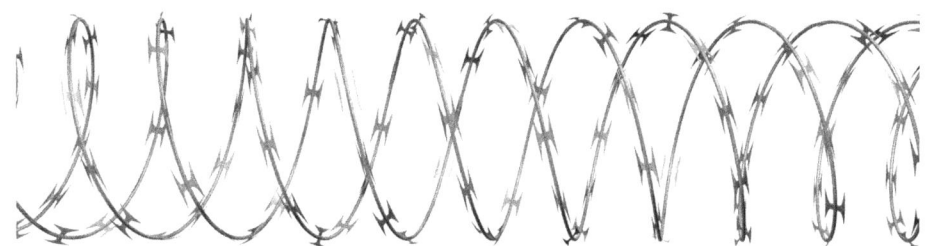

CHAPTER 34

TRASH-CAN DEBACLE

As pieces and parts continued to grow in the basement, Glen was running out of time to rid himself of this nightmare. "Come on, Jase, we need to brainstorm."

Glen pushed himself off the couch and walked around to Jason's side, swatting flies as he went. "I read somewhere—that by two people actually placing their heads together, they could collectively think as one. Come on. What do you say?"

Glen placed his hand on the side of the corpse's head and leaned down to make contact. Jason's head rolled to the side and nearly fell off as it awkwardly rested on his shoulder. He backed up a few inches, "Now, just look at you."

Glen sighed, "If you didn't want to try my idea, all you had to do is say so." Glen carefully righted the soft, putrid maggot-infested head. "Come on, let's try it again."

With both hands now holding Jason's head in place, Glen softly placed his forehead next to a festering hole that used to be Jason's ear. "O—my— God! Why didn't we think of this sooner?" Glen said as thousands of shiny winged demons dive-bombed his head and face, trying to kill the giant who just disrupted their peaceful little world.

Irritated yet somehow becoming slightly immune to their desperate assaults, Glen excitedly barked, "Slow down, slow down, I can't keep up." As nervously he bounced from one foot to the other, with his forehead still held in place.

"Okay, okay, wait, back up, I like that last one. Yeah, that one, ooh, that's good. Ya see, Jase, together we can conquer the world." Glen slowly released Jason's head, being extra careful to keep it upright.

"Important question is when's trash day?" After a pause, "I guess I shouldn't be surprised. It's not like you've answered any of my other questions.

"What? No, no, you're not getting all the credit for that. We thought of it together. Wait, wasn't that neighbor rolling trash cans?"

Glen walked to the window and looked down the block. One lone large plastic can sat curbside three or four houses down. "Um, was that always there? A bill. Gloria has to have bills somewhere.

He headed to the kitchen to begin his search. Glen chuckled as he stared through the threshold for what feels like the first time. Tile pieces shined through the cracked dried gore-covered floor, exposing the Martha Stewart house beneath. This and a wall clock that was splattered with blood from Glen's failed finger disposal plan were the only evidence anything civilized ever resided there.

After a thorough search and coming up empty-handed, Glen once again plopped down on the couch and said, "Come on, buddy, you have to help me here."

Glen sighed, "What? You're right once again, my friend. What was I thinking; of course, I don't want to do it around here."

Four minutes of rest later, in which he probably inhaled more flies than oxygen, Glen pushed himself off the couch, found his keys, and headed for his car. His dashboard clock read 7:45 as he mindlessly drifted from block to block, finally rounding a corner, and there they were. Two, three, and four sets of assorted trash cans—all glistening with early-morning dew.

As Glen sat and watched, an old lady in a robe, and a suited businessman, with his BMW idling nearby, rolled their waste to the curb. "Perfect," Glen murmured.

He went directly home and stared in awe as he pondered the stretched plastic bags and the enormous pile of swollen rotting parts. "I just don't get it. Why do they keep growing?"

No matter what he did, the stench, the flies, the gore got bigger and bigger with every passing minute of every day. He triple-bagged selected parts that were now too disfigured to identify and carried them up the once super-slippery non-forgiving steps, falling only once or twice after dribbles of gore obstructed his way.

Winded, after placing the bags, four in all, next to the front door, he found his usual spot next to his friend and said, "now we wait."

"What for?

"Nightfall, of course. What do you think— people aren't gonna notice me filling their cans in the middle of the day? Ya know, for a smart guy, sometimes you make me wonder."

Glen dozed as he watched the clock slowly tick by.

"Don't you ever sleep?" He asked Jason between nods. "What are you, some kind of superhuman or something?"

At 1:00 a.m., he did a drive-by to assess the situation. Three interior lights shined from the checkerboard houses that so casually hid behind the neatly placed cans.

"I better give it a few more minutes," Glen said out loud to himself as he slowly drove away.

Two more hours trickled by before the clock finally read 3:00.

"I'm doing it. I know, I know, I know, shut up! I'm running out of time, and it's now or never!

"Look, if all you're going to do is sit there and criticize, maybe you should keep your opinion to yourself?"

Glen silently slipped out the front door with a drooping black plastic bag swinging from his hand. 'The trunk? No, the passenger floorboard will be fast and easier.' He carefully placed the contents then hurried back for two more.

With all four bags now hogging the entire passenger floor, Glen hopped behind the wheel and drove away. What he believed to be clear across town was actually less than two miles away. As he circled the block, he sighed with relief when he saw the dark sleeping houses of the many day-dwelling people.

He killed his lights and coasted to a stop a few yards behind a large, seldom used RV. Glen paused, basically to see if anyone stirred. Second, by second, his body throbbed to the erratic beat of his heart as he sat frozen in place, staring out the windshield.

Finally, deciding loitering was doing more harm than good, he anxiously cracked his door. Glen's bald head shined like the moon when the car's dome light sprang to life, illuminating what felt like the entire block. The peace and tranquility were shattered as his door buzzer screamed through the night, sending dog after dog in a spastic frenzy from one block to the next, as far as the ear could hear.

Glen gathered up three bags. One, if not both, were dripping gore all over his car as he dragged them up, over, and across the center console.

With no time to waste, he raced to the first cluster of neatly placed cans, set a bag down, and opened the lid. It was full to the brim. Next in line was a green recycle can, "How did I not see that?" Glen whispered to himself, which lit back up the very few dogs that had stopped barking.

Third in line was a half-full old, slightly dented metal can that had definitely seen better days. Glen placed two bags in and set the lid back in place before checking the last in line, which was once again full.

Quickly, he fast stepped it down the block to the next set of cans, leaving a stinky dark trail as he went. First shot, less than half full, he dropped the dripping bag in and hustled back to his car. With the last shinny wet bag in hand, he crawled out of the driver's seat and spun around, just as a garage door [almost directly] across the street started to open.

Light shined as the door went up, revealing an idling midsize car within. A short, stocky man turned and stared once the door was secured in place.

In a panic, Glen swung the bags back over the center console, snagging it on the gear shift. He pulled, then yanked.

Suddenly, the plastic bag burst like a water balloon, sending its disgusting, putrid gory content everywhere.

"Excuse me, can I help you with something?" The man, now less than ten feet away, asked.

Glen pushed the torn sack toward the passenger seat and quickly splashed down in the gore, instantly soaking his clothes.

"Excuse me," the man said, a little more aggressively, as he kept closing the gap between them. Glen slammed his car door, turned the key, and raced away, leaving the confused, curious man standing in the street. On the verge of hyperventilating, Glen nearly lost control of his car as his tires screamed for mercy all the way home.

"Don't start on me, Jason," Glen whined as he came through the front door.

"What?" Glen paused.

"No, it didn't go so good, well… I guess it went okay. I mean, I got rid of three bags, but I messed up my car and almost got caught."

Glen plopped down on the couch and said, "Once again, Jase, I really could have used some help," before falling into a deep sleep, right next to his best and only friend.

Less than two hours later, choking, he coughed up a throat full of flies. After a brief shower, just to get him going, Glen decided to do a drive-by to assess the situation. Birds sang as the early morning dew slowly slid off the local vegetation.

He opened his driver's door. Splashed across the passenger side window and half the dash was the dark pungent gore as it slowly dripped its way to the floor. Disgusted, he slammed the door and went to get the keys to Gloria's car that still sat lifeless in the driveway. The engine barely turned over before springing to life.

Glen found himself wondering, "How long have I been here?" "What day is it?" "What month is it?" Think Glen! ....

"I'm not even sure the year? What's happened to me?" He held his head in his hands and exhaled through his teeth before driving away.

With dawn light guiding his way, the short commute took mere minutes. Glen's jaw hit the floorboard when he rounded the corner and saw trash strewed from one end of the street to the other. People stood, some still in night clothes, others in full attire, most with their arms folded across their midsection, as if trying to deflect the goosebumps that ran up and down their arms.

Two police cruisers sat in the street with their lights flashing from red to blue. One officer strung yellow police tape, another placed orange cones, while two more were escorting a lady wearing light blue slippers with matching robe in cuffs to the back seat of their car.

Stunned, Glen placed the car in reverse and slowly backs away. A horn sounded. Glen hit his brakes, nearly running right into the Channel 6 news crew, who were just arriving at the scene.

He turned on his radio to hear the news—"Big story, human body parts scattered about, by a dog, raccoon, possum whatever, basically defiling a rural southern California middle-class neighborhood," then turned it off.

Once clear of the chaos, Glen rushed home to confide in Jason, his buddy. Glen's jaw hit the ground a second time as he screeched to a stop and found his front door blowing in the breeze.

"What the ...? I couldn't have left that open." He quickly jumped out and rushed through the gaping threshold, closing the door behind him.

"Jason, Jason, you have got to start being more careful! What if some maniac saw our house wide-open and came in here to hurt you?"

"What?"

"No, I'm not. I just don't want to see you get hurt, is all."

"We're not going to argue about it! Now hurry, turn on the TV."

Glen waited a few seconds.

"Okay then, I'll get it. You have got to be one of the laziest people I think I have ever met."

Glen surfed through several channels before coming to rest on a local news station.

"BREAKING NEWS," covered the screen.

"Authorities have reported human remains have been found scattered across a public street just a few blocks from Rosecrans Boulevard. Our Channel 6 anchor reporter, John Stone, is live on the scene.—"John, what's going on out there?"

"Well, Dan, what we have so far is this. Police Sergeant Michael Alhen has told us that this morning, around 5:00 a.m., several neighbors reported what appeared to be human body parts scattered across this city street." The reporter moved aside as he waved his free hand.

"Apparently, at least one person is in custody at this time. We're not sure if they have been charged or if there has been or ever will be any other arrests."

Glen turned the TV off.

"I know, but I don't want to see anymore."

Glen carefully sat down on the edge of the couch, with his hands folded in his lap.

"I can't sit here and let some innocent poor old lady get in trouble for what I've done."

Glen looked at his friend with surprise, "What do you mean, what am I gonna do?"

"Well, I'm not sure, but I have to do something." Glen pondered.

"I don't understand, *who* will take you away?"

"Why do you say that?"

"Yeah."

"I see."

"No… we don't want that to happen."

"Okay, okay, I get it."

Glen got up with his head bowed in shame as he dragged his feet all the way to his bed, where he fell into a deep, depressed sleep.

Special investigator Sergeant Vince Kirk with the San Diego Southern District Police Department Homicide Division meticulously gathered the parts from off the beach, just adjacent to the Mexican border, and carefully placed them in sealed plastic bags.

This came after numerous calls were placed by traumatized, early-morning beachgoers.

"So, what do you think?" his sidekick, Detective Johnson asked, while blowing the steam to cool his coffee.

"I think this is one very sick, very unlucky son of a bitch. Less than 100 feet, 100 feet, and they would have been in Mexico. Even the storm was working against him. Usually, Mexico washes up in San Diego, not vice versa."

"What do you make of the parts?"

"Well, we have what looks like assorted parts of possibly several people. Hard to tell right now."

After placing the bags in a large cooler, Detective Kirk stared out to sea.

"Sir, are we done here?"

"Ya know, Johnson, the world has gone to hell, and it would really be nice, just once, to stop one of these sick bastards *before* they killed any people."

"Yeah, I think that might be another department, sir."

"I guess you're probably right. Come on, let's get out of here."

Back at the precinct, while Detective Kirk was checking Glen's ice cooler into the property room, Detective Carson approached.

"Excuse me, sir, can I see that ice chest?"

"Of course, mind if I ask why?" Kirk asked as he stepped aside.

"Well, sir, I think I may know where this cooler came from, and I have his address."

"Really. And how did you come across this?"

Detective Carson explained the entire situation, complete with how he helped load the cooler onto the boat.

"Okay, let's get a search warrant, and meanwhile, let's send a couple detectives, me and whoever, over for a friendly visit."

Carson perked up, "I'll volunteer, sir."

Unable to scale the back fence unnoticed, Glen walked to his car with the pistol neatly tucked away under his black jacket. He cruised the whole block twice before coming to rest about four houses down from his target. Feeling a little overconfident, when he probably should have been nervous, Glen got out and walked the short distance, stopping only when he came to the little blue car, Evelyn's car.

He paused briefly before making his way down the side of their garage, hoping to slip through a rear entrance without catching the nosey lady's attention. His heart began to pound as soon as he stepped on their property. He squatted and patted the gun. *I'm in control here. I don't need to be nervous.*

Pressing himself against the wall, he continued down the side and round the corner. He could now see his Dad's house, truck, and boat. The lady was probably peering through one of the top floor windows directly over him.

He carefully slinked by, reaching the door in seconds. Nervously, he raised his shaking hand to the doorknob and found it to be unlocked. Glen slowly opened the door. Like a cat stalking its prey, he slipped inside and carefully closed the door behind him.

Even Detective Carson, who wasn't assigned to homicide, recognized the horrible stench of decaying death the second they pulled up to Glen's house, as he unsnapped his gun on the way to the front door.

"Easy now, I'll call for backup." After doing so, both detectives stood to the side as Kirk rang the bell. Nothing happened. He tried a second time, nothing. Carson racked his knuckles against the door, still no reply.

Kirk tried the knob, and to both their surprise, it was open.

At first, they thought they heard a generator in the distance.

Flies swarmed through the barely cracked door.

With their guns drawn and their shirts held covering the lower half of their faces, both men cautiously pushed their way into Glen's little house of horrors.

"Evelyn"

"Yes," she said with her eyes glued to the back house.

"I was just checking if you went outside," George said, as he slowly reached for his 9mm semi-automatic pistol, which has seldom been more than three feet away since his return from the Korean War. Not only was George sure he heard the door, but he also felt the climate change. Being a retired army Captain with three purple hearts and more brass than he could count, George definitely was no rookie when it came to battle.

Glen smelled the long-lost pleasant aroma of home cooking, *maybe a pot roast?* as he crept down the hallway with his gun held high. He heard a television. *Gilligan's Island*, it sounded like, coming from a room five feet away on his left.

"What's that smell? Did you pass gas?" Evelyn asked.

No one replied.

"George?"

Still no reply.

Glen paused at the doorway, then quickly jumped through the opening with his gun held with both hands in front of him. The TV was indeed on *Gilligan's Island*. Two empty recliners, one being a little larger than the other, sat facing the set.

Glen lowered his gun a few inches.

"George." The lady's voice was coming Glen's way.

Choking, the two officers waded through torrents of flies. When they came to the living room, they gasped. On the couch, surrounded by mounds of spoiled food and trash, sat the decaying corpse of what appeared to be a male, although it was hard to tell. His face was completely missing, leaving only a white skull and remnants of cartilage behind. Where the eyes, nose, and mouth used to be, now swam puddles of withering maggots.

Unable to imagine anything worse, the officers pressed forward with their guns at the ready, hoping backup would arrive soon. The flies and odor seemed to increase as they plunged deeper into this hell. The kitchen floor was completely covered from corner to corner with dried, near-black blood.

The cupboard was open, all the under-sink items were sitting, obviously stuck to the floor. Maggots infested rotting food covered the blood-streaked table. A hose hung from the garbage disposal, draping over the counter that was covered in gore and what looked like smashed, mutilated human fingers.

On the far side of the kitchen and through a short corridor, a black blood trail ran through a half-open door that millions of flies were coming from.

Reluctant to not further contaminate the crime scene, Detective Kirk carefully pushed the door open with his foot and the two men, after yelling one of many warnings, descended the stairs.

Three large trash bags, bloated and stretched so thin you could see through them, sat next to at least two deflated bags that had obviously popped, spilling their wicked contents onto the floor. Three piles. One large, a medium, and a small, of human parts sat semi–neatly stacked amongst the organs and gore that flowed from the popped bags.

The most disturbing thing, if there could be one, would have to be the seven heads, hanging by a wire through their noses and out their mouths, in a neat little line, all staring at the rafters, with nearly dried gore hanging about a foot off each one.

Nothing in these detectives' training and or experiences could have prepared them for this level of mayhem. They stood at the bottom of the stairs in complete shock, swatting flies and staring, their stomachs turning. The morning's coffee and donuts now stung the back of their throats.

Finally, content there was nothing living to save here, the detectives headed back up the stairs ... as fast as their legs could take them.

Suddenly a high–pitched squeal cut through Glen's head as he turned with the gun still held high and saw the lady, the one who followed him to Home Depot, the one who watches his every move from her upstairs porch was now standing off to his side, screaming to high heaven.

Everything went into super-fast mode.

Someone jumped him and hollered, "Evelyn, run!"

Glen's gun went off. He didn't mean to fire it; it just went off—sending a bullet straight through the wall, on his way to the ground.

Evelyn continued to scream.

Glen wrestled with the man, hitting him twice in the head with his gun.

George's gun discharged into the ceiling.

Glen wrestled free and ran. George fired. It felt like a baseball bat had struck Glen from behind as the bullet ripped through his shoulder. Glen fired over his back as he ran for the door. George took cover. Evelyn never stopped screaming.

The detectives heard screaming and gunshots coming from what sounded like the backyard. They bolted towards the noise. Once outside, they heard two more gunshots and more screaming, all coming from a neighbor's house.

Detective Kirk ran for the squad car and his shotgun. The younger Detective Carson ran to scale the fence, straight into disaster.

Fueled by adrenalin, Glen couldn't feel his shoulder as he continued to fire all the way out the door. George fired two more shots; one struck the door frame, the other grazed Glen's leg, causing him to stumble as he regained composure and leaped for the fence.

At the same instant, Detective Carson also jumped the fence. Neither man could see each other until it was too late.

Of all the places they could have crossed that fence, they chose the same spot, at the same time. They came together—head-to-head—in mid-air.

Glen, with his vision now blurred from the collision, tumbled into his yard and fired two more shots toward his new attacker, who ironically was now on the opposite side of the fence.

After hitting the ground, Carson returned fire, piercing the wood fence three times, catching Glen once in the left arm.

Panicked, injured, and bleeding—Glen ran.

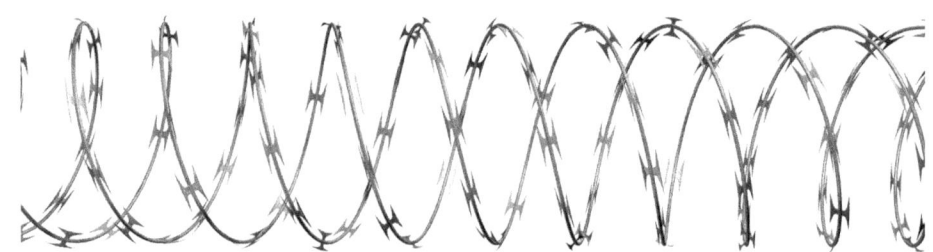

CHAPTER 35

RIOT

I pushed Glen's file, which I could barely put down, to the side and went to the yard. Everybody was grouping. No one was alone. Even the screws knew something was about to go down, all doubled up in the towers and walking three to five deep on the yard. The tension was so thick; you could cut it with a knife. I found my homeboys in their usual spot, watching everything everyone did, including the guards.

"Dave, glad to see you back, dawg," Moose said, as soon as I walked up.

I already knew the next question, so I answered it. "Fuckin' Warden, or Captain, who knows, stuck me in the hole for five miserable days. What's up out here?"

Moose explained the situation in detail, with the only surprising part being the white guy was one of our homeboys. Not that it mattered in this particular situation, but it certainly didn't help.

"So, tomorrow morning?"

"Yeah, that's the plan."

"Knives or fist?" I asked.

"Not sure, just be ready."

Glen would be excluded. Seldom did an old lifer who wasn't involved in the mix have anything to do with such problems. I, myself, wasn't quite so fortunate.

Like every other white and probably black as well, I spent the weary late-night hours preparing for the dreaded morning that we all wished would never come. Preparation meaning, basically picking your thing and grinding a nice fresh razor-sharp edge to whatever weapon you possess. Glen read his book as I carefully sharpened my blade or "bone crusher," as one of this size was called, across the concrete floor.

Finally finished, I laid back on my rack and thought about my wife. Did she deserve this? Do I have a choice? People will die tomorrow, and I need to focus on making sure I'm not one of them.

"I'm sorry, babe," I whispered in the dark.

Morning came all too soon. I woke to large black shadows lurking past my door. Maybe they were getting a headcount on participants or possibly trying to intimidate. I'm not sure.

I skipped breakfast. Armed and booted, my heart pulsated throughout my whole body. This was one of those things; no matter how many times you did it, you still couldn't get used to it. Well, I couldn't anyway.

I came out of my cell. The dayroom was basically empty, except for a few lifers who had seen it too many times to be entertained. One such individual was Glen, who simply said, "be careful."

The indoor gunner sat in the tower with his AR-15 resting in his lap. When we made eye contact, he smiled a mysterious grin but continued to sit.

In all the time I had been there, I couldn't recall a time the gunner sat down. Not one.

"Have fun," the smiling floor cop said on my way through the dayroom.

The inner sally port door closed the second I came through it, sending a message of no return. I paused, subconsciously hoping the outer door would close, trapping me in—no such luck.

I nervously pushed forward, pumped out my chest, somehow calmed myself, and quickly stepped through the port. Before my eyes had time to adjust to the early morning sun, pandemonium broke out everywhere. People ran at each other from all directions, except the Mexicans, who were simply trying to get out of the way.

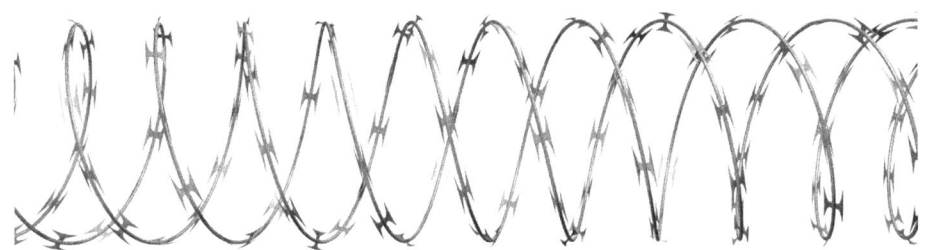

CHAPTER 36

SWAT

The cruiser came to a sliding stop. Detective Kirk jumped out with his shotgun in hand and heard three more shots coming from what he believed to be the backyard.

His police instinct, combined with the unfortunate possibility that his partner could be down, overrode any and all fears. He raced down the side of the garage, straight through an open gate, and saw his partner pulling himself off the ground, pointing at the fence.

Suddenly, two rounds ripped through the cedar boards. Both cops hit the ground.

After firing two more times, Glen slammed the back door and ran to secure the front, which hung wide open. "Jason." He yelled, "Jason, are you okay?" He once again waited for a reply. "They're after us, buddy. I think they're trying to kill us."

Within minutes police had surrounded the house.

"We have you surrounded. Put down your weapons and slowly come out of the house." An officer said through a blow horn.

Glass shattered as Glen fired twice right through the window.

While running for cover, the police returned fire, breaking even more windows.

Glen hit the ground with his hands covering his ears as wood, plaster, and glass hailed down on him.

The shooting finally stopped.

Daylight seeped through the many holes the officers just punched through the house, enhancing the flies, smoke, and dust that seemed to linger, froze in mid-air. Clinging to the floor, Glen crawled away from the window.

"Jason, buddy, we're gonna be okay."

Winded, Glen propped Jason back to a sitting position. Hunched low to the floor, he went to find his gas mask and fresh ammunition. While doing so, he glanced out a window and saw a large black armored truck angling sideways in the street, with SWAT blasted down its side.

Dressed to the hilt, agents with big guns jumped out and quickly took cover.

Sitting on the carpet, with his back to the couch, Glen was reloading his gun when he heard '*thump, thump*,' followed by the canisters that, bounced across the floor, and blew up. Not just blew up, but exploded his whole world, as white light—so intense, it completely blinded him, followed by a sound like nothing Glen had ever imagined in his life.

He squinted his eyes really tight and grabbed his ears with both hands as he fell to the side in agonizing pain.

He could feel more canisters exploding but couldn't see or hear them.

He pulled his hands from his ears; they were wet. He assumed it was blood but wasn't sure if it came from his shoulder, arm, leg, or ears.

He felt his way to the clip just as his vision returned. After snapping the clip in, he fired three shots toward the front door. Then quickly secured the gas mask in place.

SWAT returned fire for what seemed like days. In reality, it was a full five minutes.

"Ceasefire," the commanding agent finally said.

"Mr. Sombers, are you in there?"

Glen's ears were still ringing so loud, he couldn't quite make out the words, but he knew they were saying something.

"Are you surrendering on your own accord?"

Glen fired one shot wildly through the air.

The agents hunkered down but didn't open fire.

The front door hung by splinters still attached to the hinges. All the front windows had been shot out. The walls looked like Swiss cheese.

Glen looked up and saw Jason once again had fallen to the side. He carefully straightened him back up.

Time passed.

Glen's hearing, hampered by a continual ring, did indeed return. His whole body ached, but his shoulder and arm, which were still bleeding, hurt like hell.

His leg had a pretty bad cut from the graze, but his shoulder was the main problem. Glen feared he may bleed to death. More time passed.

The agents killed his power hours ago, and the sun was now going down. Seeking resolution, Glen heard, "Mr. Sombers, I'm Special Agent Captain Frost, with San Diego's SWAT team. You have ten minutes to surrender, or we're coming in to get you."

Glen reached for his mask and secured it in place. Then he checked his weapon to make sure it was fully loaded.

On the tenth minute, Captain Frost gave one final warning, "Mr. Sombers, this is your last chance. Come out now with your hands behind your head."

Several seconds passed while Glen shoved little rolled-up pieces of couch stuffing deep down his ears.

'*Thump, thump.*' Multiple canisters bounced across the floor. Some *flash-bangs* (again), others tear gas. Within seconds the room was filled with smoke, visibility was zero.

Glen fired two shots toward the front, hoping this would hold them off. More canisters exploded. Glen continued to breathe through his mask. He seemed to be adjusting to their assault. Even the bright light was becoming more bearable as he squinted his eyes to each eruption.

"I could do this all day," he hollered inside his mask; of course, no one heard him.

Suddenly, he thought of Jason, '*How is he possibly breathing in this?*'

"Jason buddy, I'm so sorry. Hold on." Glen choked as he removed the mask and started trying to place it on Jason's decayed skeletal head. The mask, of course, wouldn't seal. Its mere weight nearly pulled Jason's head off as it continually slumped forward, resting the chemical canister on what was left of his sternum.

Frustrated and coughing, with snot, mucous, and tears running down his face, Glen ran out the front door, not so much in surrender, as desperately seeking fresh air.

"Drop the gun, MOTHERFUCKER, drop the gun!"

He barely heard someone he couldn't see yelling. Half blinded, confused, and delirious from blood loss, gasping for air, Glen stumbled forward and fell off the porch.

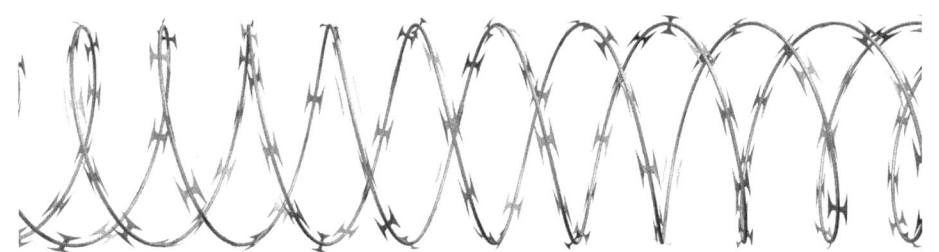

CHAPTER 37

83 STABBED, 21 SHOT, 7 DEAD

Usually, in a prison riot, you don't just run out and stab people. You fight your heart out, then when someone gets stabbed, you start stabbing. Everything changes when the blades come out, right down to the COs who, for some reason, I never will understand, stand and fight with you, Macing everybody, kicking, punching, and screaming. But when knives come out, COs clear the area, best they can, and the gunners open fire.

The part I don't get is—if two guys even look like they're gonna fight, the tower shoots them. But you can riot, shank free, all day long? This makes no sense to me.

Anyway, alarms were going off, and people, two, three hundred of them, were fighting everywhere you looked. Some were down on the ground gasping for air after being Maced; others were down holding their heads and or a broken limb or two. But the mass majority was up and fighting.

I, myself, was scrapping with two blacks—one big, one little, when I got socked from the side. I didn't see it coming. My world went black for a brief second.

As I was pulling my bloody self off the ground, two youngster homeboys ran to my rescue, and the three of us quickly laid waste to our opponents and turned to find more.

Right then, the first gunshot sounded. This being our cue. Everyone instantly was armed, and the blood began to flow.

While hacking my way through hell—*bam*—I got hit in the back. Before I could retaliate, I got stuck in the shoulder and cut in the side. Two gunners opened fire with semi-automatic weapons. Everywhere you looked, people were dropping like flies.

Suddenly, the whole yard hit the ground. It's like some kind of barbaric, prehistoric thing. The rulers or kings, let's say, go down, and everyone instantly follows suit.

The only ones standing were guards.

One of them, a sergeant, was stumbling around yelling with his arm extended over a foot and bleeding like he might die. He would later have his arm amputated, forcing him into retirement.

The towers, at least two of them, continued to shoot several seconds after we were down. This being common practice in supermax. We laid face down on the ground while COs walked around Macing and, in some cases assaulting us, while we bled, waiting for medical help.

Help eventually (that is, after a couple hours), started arriving by way of ambulance and prison medics with gurneys. Rule was, if you could walk, you didn't need any help. On this day, a CO got hurt pretty bad, and a Sergeant at that. Therefore, what little treatment we usually had coming after a riot wasn't happening.

I, myself, was eventually (again—that is, after a couple hours), scooped up and taken to the hole. I didn't see medical for nearly two weeks. By this time, I no longer needed them.

Turned out, eighty-three people were stabbed, hundreds were cut, bruised, and broken. Twenty-one were shot. Six COs were injured, with one arm amputation. A total of only seven deaths. How did only seven people die?

I don't know. Maybe the fact that all we did was eat and lift weights all day might have had something to do with it. I was thrown in a cell with someone in much worse shape than myself. His name was Doug, a.k.a. "*Doug the Thug*." Doug was a monster at six feet, five inches, 280 pounds.

To date, this quite possibly was the longest, most boring six months of my entire life. But like all things good and bad, it did indeed pass. I can honestly say, the only thing I got from it was I became a hell of an angler.

Six months to the day, I woke to the Captain once again standing at my door.

"Hey, tough guy, how ya doin' in there?"

"I'm good Captain, and you?"

"Wanna go back to the yard today?"

"Yeah, I guess."

"Okay." The Captain started to leave before turning back, "Oh, by the way, they're still on lockdown. Just thought you might want to know."

"Any word how much longer?"

"I don't know, maybe six more months or… maybe when my Sergeant's arm grows back?"

"Yeah, sorry about that, you know, shit just happens in a riot."

"Oh yeah, we know."

"Hey, any word how much time I lost?"

"Now, you know that's not my department. However, in your case, I made an exception, and we only took 90 days, which you've already earned back. Consider it like … a birthday present." He paused and smiled, "to your wife."

"Thank you, Captain."

"No problem, tough guy." He said while walking away.

In the California Department of Corrections, if you lose 90 days on a disciplinary action, you can get it back after 90 days of clean conduct. If you lose 91 days or more, it's gone forever.

Twenty minutes after the Captain walked away, my cell door popped, "Wilson, roll it up." The loudspeaker blared. Roll it up. That's funny. What do I have to roll up?" Anyway, back to the yard I went.

Confused as to where I would be living, I went to the unit office. "What do you mean, where's your cell? The same place it was."

"Are you kidding me?"

"No, can't nobody live with the cannibal. We put some youngster in there a few months back. He cried to the doctor, 'I can't sleep, *wa, wa.*' We had to move him. Same ole cell, 268 lower. He's probably waiting for you."

Glen was indeed standing by the door when I got there.

"What's up, celly? You didn't eat anybody while I was gone, did ya?"

"No, nobody to be missed anyway. How the hell are ya?" Glen asked as the door started opening.

"I'm good and glad to be back."

"Heard you got stabbed."

"Yeah, that was eons ago."

Obviously starved for companionship, Glen asked, "You ready for some Backgammon?"

"Not yet, big guy. Let me relax a minute, then I'll be glad to kick your ass."

"You… wanna watch my TV?"

"Fuck no. I don't want to watch your TV. That's just weird. Don't start getting weird on me. Seriously, though, they should be giving me my property soon."

"Wilson, report to R&R" the loudspeaker crackled… "Like right now."

Our door popped.

An hour later, I returned with all or most all my stuff. I no sooner got my things situated when all our doors opened, and the speakers barked, "Yard." And just like that, with no warning, no heads up, nothing, we were off lockdown.

People slowly emerged onto the tier. Some were stretching, others ran for the showers. After six months of lockdown, most everyone was relieved to be out of their cramped, very little six-by-ten foot cells.

I, myself? I was just happy to have clothes on. I moseyed down the tier and placed my things in line for the shower. Two hundred people were trying to get in the four-man stall. I decided I could wait. Bottom line was—all of us were going to wait—some just more patiently than others.

After securing a place in line, I went back to my cell to read. People looked at me like I was crazy as I stood in front of my door and waited for it to open.

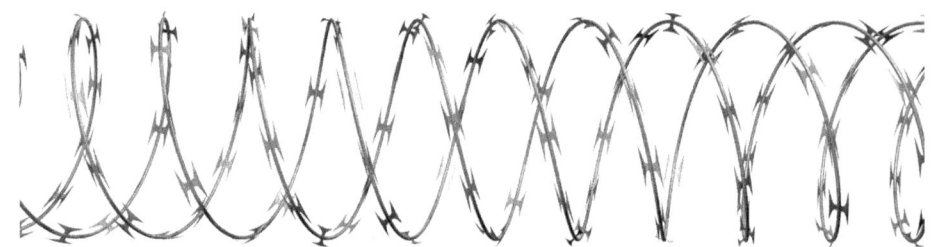

CHAPTER 38

ARRESTED, INDICTED, CONVICTED, "THE CANNIBAL"

Pain erupted through Glen's body as one agent's cleated boot pressed his head to the ground while another agent jumped, knee–first onto his back.

"Clear." One of the SWAT team members yelled as the zip ties tightened into place.

Eight agents ran into the house. At least two, not quite ready for this level of decadent decay, ran back out choking.

Within seconds Glen was yanked off the ground and rushed with every escort imaginable, including a helicopter, to the hospital.

The entire fourth floor of Alvarado hospital was reserved for Federal, State, and County inmates. On this day, the whole wing was evacuated, anticipating Glen's arrival. Wide-eyed nurses and doctors, mixed with agents from every department, state and federal alike, trimmed the walls, while Glen, after two hours in surgery, was quickly ushered down the hall.

Safely secured to the bed by both hands and feet, the police, for whatever reason, chose to cover the lower half of Glen's face with a hockey-type mask.

Back at the house, agents were absolutely astonished. Rotting human organs and parts were everywhere, from the basement to the fridge. Loaded fly–strips, thick as a man's arm, swayed in the breeze. The kitchen, once the flies were clear, actually had eerie ghost-like human faces resting in plates of rotting food.

The basement had to be the worse, although it was a hard call. The entire scene was like nothing any of the agents had ever seen or even trained for.

The police held the news crews (hungry for a shot of the action) at bay while they collected samples and took pictures of what could quite possibly be the goriest crime scene in San Diego's recorded history.

Jason—he was a star. More pictures were taken of him, sitting there in his WWII single canister chemical gas mask, than John Wayne himself.

Across town, when detectives kicked–in Glen's door, they too were a bit bewildered to find the whole inside had started to grow, literally. Some kind of grey and green moss grew from everything. The walls, the furniture, the floor, everything.

After calling HazMat (the California Hazardous Material Unit) to the scene, they located the source of the contamination and treated it like one of the deadliest cocktails on earth, which it quite possibly was.

The room was a mass of growing, smelly fungi that stretched from ceiling to floor. The bucket, once they finally got to it, still sat where and how Glen left it weeks before. Its crystalline substance is no longer bright and clear but now a rainbow of colors ranging from red to blues and everything in-between.

All neighbors within an eight-mile radius were evacuated, creating even more media hype. The whole thing was a catastrophe of Biblical proportions.

Glen's hand and foot irons were replaced with heavy nylon straps as he wiggled night and day, yelling something about a person named Jason. No one could figure it out. Once his shoulder and arm wounds stabilized, Glen was transferred to the San Diego County jail, where an entire wing had been designated, just for him.

Still suffering from delusion, he didn't understand why he couldn't just stay in the hospital where the food was better and the people, although frightened, seemed a little nicer.

Charged with multiple counts of murder, he lived in the same cell for the next three years, coming out only for court, to see his attorney, or an occasional doctor visit.

The justice department can get away with this simply because county jail is classified as a "temporary housing unit," so they are exempt from the rules and regulations that govern a permanent housing facility. In other words, "the man" can literally do anything they want. Who ya gonna tell?

The prosecutor, of course, was seeking the death penalty. Glen's defense team fought tooth and nail against it. As mentioned earlier, in order to convict someone of a crime, they have to be "sane at the time the crime was committed." Glen was obviously crazy as a bag of angry monkeys when he killed those people, as well as now, months later, sitting in the county's jail cell, talking to some imaginary friend named Jason.

During this time, the prosecution arranged to have Glen evaluated by multiple doctors. At least three of whom actually swore under oath that in their professional opinions, they found Mr. Sombers (as they referred to Glen, the accused) to be 100% sane then and now—strapped from head to toe on a utility dolly, staring through a hockey-mask. Each time he went to court, he was secured in this manner.

Crowd control was a big issue. Sometimes the feds would cancel their court proceedings, which were intended for the daily mass of immigrants, San Diego being a border city, and allow access to their tunnels, which for certain high-profile state cases ... Glen's case being the top of this list. Other times, he would be flown by helicopter, hopping from building to building.

When they moved him by van, they would close the surrounding street, using police roadblocks.

No matter how he went, he was always strapped to the dolly and laid down like cargo once onboard. The silly little white hockey mask was always in place, no matter how far he was going. Unable to grasp why they were acting this way, Glen, for the first time in his life, truly felt like a monster.

"What did you plan to do with the remaining body parts?" One of the more rational shrinks, a Dr. Roy Springer, asked.

"I, well actually, Jason and I, were going to eat them."

There it was, just like that, he became "The Cannibal."

Every news station across the nation was all over it. In Glen's mind, he was just being the crazy monster they were treating him like.

Esquire and some other even less worthy rags were having an absolute field day with it. "The Cannibal this." "The Cannibal that." "Today the Cannibal ...." It went on and on.

Some even went as far as stating, "The Cannibal was planning on killing and eating the President and his family." People ate it up (pardon the expression) like apple pie. A short thirteen years after the Manson murders and equally gruesome, the hype grew like weeds.

Displeased with the attention and careful not to create another Manson-like hero, the government killed the story shortly after Glen was sentenced.

Thirteen reliable, competent doctors declared Glen, who stared at them over his hockey mask, to be absolutely insane at the time the murders were committed. Whereas only three quacks (hired, of course, by the government), said under oath they found Glen—the Cannibal, the monster, the crazy-as-a-bag-of-monkeys guy—to be sane, then, now, and always.

The prosecutor was losing ground, and he knew it. If Glen was found to be insane, he could not face murder charges and he would be sent to a hospital, where he would live a pretty good life until he was finally declared to be sane, at which time he could be released back into society.

This was completely unacceptable in the government's view and in most of America's eyes. The new offer, in return for a guilty plea, would be eight consecutive life sentences, with no possibility of parole. Glen didn't understand this, stating, "How do they figure? Jason is absolutely fine! Ask him. He'll tell ya."

He refused the deal. "I'm not going to plea to killing someone who isn't dead. Besides, he's my friend." They went back and forth until the prosecutor came up with this brainy idea.

"Okay, how 'bout we drop one charge of murder regarding the neighbor lady, simply because your client had no idea she was even there. Whatever you need to tell Mr. Sombers is on you."

"That might work. I'll get back to you in a day or two."

Glen agreed, "See, I told you he was fine."

After twenty-two motions, ranging from change of venue to my oatmeal was cold, which resulted in too many trips to court to count, and over three years of county jail, Glen was eventually sentenced to serve seven, not eight consecutive life sentences. Hungry for the death penalty, the prosecutor was greatly disappointed, stating, "I'm sorry to the families and all of America. But please understand, I did my best."

Glen transferred to Corcoran State Prison, where he would live for the next five years, in what is classified as the Security Housing Unit, better known as the SHU program. This program is designated for long-term segregation for disciplinary reasons. Unfortunately for Glen, it's also used for high-profile inmates, which he definitely was.

After three long miserable years of being locked down 24/7 in county jail and another five years of total isolation in the SHU program, Glen was transferred to Folsom State Prison and, shortly thereafter, released to its general prison population.

He, along with others, was then transferred out of their older prisons to the brand-new, Calipatria, sometime after it opened in 1992.

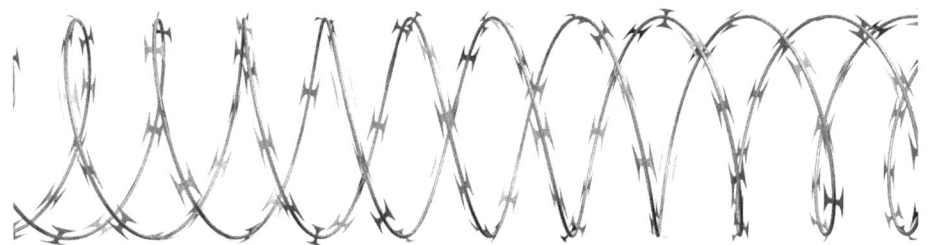

CHAPTER 39

THE CANNIBAL'S LAST HURRAH

Glen returned from the shower. I was only a few guys back, so out I went. After a really hot refreshing cleansing, in which I scrubbed until my skin nearly bled, I too returned to the cell.

"Wait, no, I won't. Be quiet. Someone's going to hear you." I heard Glen say as I approached the door.

My first thought was, "who's in my cell?" My second was, "oh no." When I peered through the door and saw Glen standing by himself in the middle of the room.

"You okay in there, buddy?" I asked before the door opened.

Glen spun and stared, never saying a word.

"I don't know how the hell you live with that crazy bastard; he's been doing weird shit for days," said the guard, who approached with keys in hand.

The door opened, Glen stood stupid and stared.

"Glen, you okay?"

I asked a little louder than probably needed.

Glen's glazed–over eyes seemed to focus for the first time. "Yeah, I'm fine, and you?"

He looked around the room as if he just realized he was standing right in the way and quickly jumped on his rack. Sensing my concern, he grabbed a book, which he held upside-down and pretended to read.

"Wow," I muttered to myself before getting dressed and ready for the yard.

After an awkward forty-nine minutes, the cell opened.

"You're not going out?" I asked on my way through the door. He didn't even lower his book. I paused, being the COs wait for no one. I stepped through the opening and rushed to the sally port.

After a couple uneventful hours (uneventful being just one fistfight in the only blind spot on the yard and no shooting or stabbings), in which time I completed my workout, and headed back inside.

Cool thing about a long-term lockdown is no one's strung out, well, not strung out on contraband heroin anyway. Ya, see, here's the thing. If you go to the prison shrink—who no longer has a medical license to practice in the free world—and tell him you're having problems sleeping at night, *alá* "I'm having a hard time sleeping," then he or she will prescribe enough dope to drop an elephant. Then each day or in some cases two to three times a day, this pill cart comes to you and gives you the dope for free!

I don't get it. Here we are, most of us in prison for *selling* dope. Then you come to prison, and they give you *free dope*? Wow, who'd thought?

Anyway, as I came through the sally port, an officer said, "Wilson." So, I stepped out of line.

"Yeah, boss?"

"You need to talk to your celly. I'm about to lock him up."

189

"Gotcha, boss," I said on my way to the stairs.

Glen stood once again in the middle of the cell, talking to himself. This time, buck–naked.

"Glen, what the fuck you doing, homey?"

"Fine, and you?"

"I'm good. Where's your clothes, dawg?"

He quickly looked down threw his hands up in a futile attempt to cover himself while he vigilantly searched his surrounding area for his clothes.

Minutes later, when the door opened, he was dressed and, on his bed, once again buried in his book, like nothing ever happened.

"Look, dude, you're acting fuckin' weird, and you need to get your shit together. How long have you been this way?"

"What way?"

"Standing around fuckin' naked, talking to yourself and shit, come on now."

He stared.

"Cops talking about locking your ass up. Now, how long you been this way?"

Glen jumped off his rack, nearly landing on me, and rushed the door.

"Which cop?"

"I don't know which one."

"He's been messing with me for days, weeks even."

"Dude, would you like to see the doctor?" I knew this was silly the second I said it, and so did Glen. They generally don't give meds or treatment to people who genuinely need it, only the ones who say they can't sleep.

"Why so they can laugh at me or maybe put me on some pill I don't need? No, thank you. I'm good. That cop's the problem!"

With his story basically complete and nothing left much worth reading, I asked, "You wanna play backgammon until dinner time?"

"Backgammon, what?"

He looked back at me like it was the first time he had ever heard the word.

"Backgammon? No, I'm okay. But thank you for asking." He climbed back on his rack.

Worried and a little weirded out, I let it go and started preparing for chow.

"You're not going to dinner?"

"Dinner?"

"Yeah, are you going to chow?"

Glen paused and looked at me like it may be some kind of setup. "Chow? No, I think I'm okay."

"Whatever. You need to quit acting so fuckin' weird, though."

With no reply, his head slightly nodded up and down as he continued to stare.

Things were getting downright strange. I mean, living with someone in an six-by-ten cell who committed multiple homicides was scary enough, but now he wants to start acting up? This was unacceptable, to say the least.

I stayed outside until yard recall, at sunset. Then I used the dayroom until lock-up at 9:00 p.m.

Glen never left the cell, and every time I swung by there, he was standing in the middle talking and even arguing with himself. On one pass by, I heard him yelling back and forth with someone named Jason. Go figure.

My neighbor was standing at his door, shaking his head from side to side as I approached.

Now, when a cop says, "Lock him up," he's usually referring to suicide watch. 'Suicide watch' is a situation where you're stripped of your clothes and placed in a rubber–padded room. At night you're wrapped in a shipping blanket with Velcro restraints. Truly a prison inside of prison. One in which I wouldn't wish on my worst enemy.

So, to have Glen locked up is a very big step. I, myself, wasn't prepared to take.

Glen spun around, still mumbling to himself.

"Yes."

"You okay?"

Failing to answer, he crawled up on his bed and grabbed his book.

"I'm telling ya, Wilson," the CO said, as he came down the tier, "If he doesn't straighten up, I'm locking him up."

That night, I woke a thousand times to him mumbling in his sleep, often yelling out, waking his own self. Always the same brainless bullshit, Jason this, Jason that. It went on and on. Then when I finally did fall asleep, I woke to light flashing across my eyes.

Looking up, I saw Glen's taller-than-life figure standing at the door, swaying from side to side, casting shadows all over the cell.

"Dude, what are you doing?"

He turned and stared for ten, maybe twenty seconds, then he would crawl back on his bed, never saying a word. This happened numerous times.

The following morning, after a restless night's sleep, I woke to the sound of cells opening and Glen once again standing at the door, bouncing from foot to foot, mumbling.

Nearly late for work, I pulled myself up a few inches.

Glen glanced over his shoulder and said, "I got this Jason,— you just sit there and smile." He turned back around impatiently, waiting for the door to open. The second it did, Glen jumped through the opening. I saw something shiny in his hand. I quickly sat up.

"Glen… no."

Before I could react further, he mounted the officer, the same one from the day before, and began stabbing him across his head, back, and shoulders.

I jumped up all too late as the MI6 ripped the morning calm to pieces. The first two shots tore through Glen's torso.

The third took off his jaw and part of his face. The fourth hit him high on the shoulder. Glen continued his assault, completely unphased until the fifth and final shot, square to his head.

Glen fell on top of the lifeless officer. Both men void of any living soul. Time froze as carbon smoke slowly dissipated, leaving only ringing ears behind.

I don't know if you've ever been in a small concrete building when an M16 went off, but believe me, there are no words to describe it. Defeated and splashed with Glen's last thought or lack thereof, I slowly wiped the gore from my face and stumbled backward onto my bunk. I truly believe a lifer goes home the day he dies, but Glen? He had problems, serious problems, and the officer? I understand he died in the line of duty, but the entire situation had me rocked to my center's core.

Six weeks later, I paroled to the loving arms of my wife, who had patiently stood by and waited loyally all these years. This was truly one of the happiest days of both our lives.

THE END

EPILOGUE

As I now sit in Federal prison about to be released again to my wife's loving arms, I'm not sure if I have ever mentally healed from my visit to Calipatria State Prison twenty-three years ago. Most all supermax facilities are volatile. But none of them held a candle to Calipat. It was and possibly still is absolutely the worse of the worst.

ABOUT THE AUTHOR

DAVID WILSON

Born and raised with his four siblings in San Diego California, via a brief three-year stent in Alaska, and a few summers in Arkansas with his father, and his family. David considers himself a true San Diegan.

There's no "Class of" for Mr. Wilson, being he barely made it through the eighth grade, stepping out of society at a very young age, and somehow saw his thirty-third birthday before his first prison term.

Since then, he has drifted in and out of both state and federal prison, covering all custody levels, totaling four terms, serving seventeen or so years of his life behind bars.

Now at sixty-two years of age, and recently released from Federal Prison, he currently resides in Sacramento California, where Robin, his wife of twenty-six years, landed—shortly after the judge's mallet struck oak this last time.

A cancer survivor, David enjoys relaxing by the pool with Robin and their cats, Messy and Waldo.